HARDCASE HALLORAN

Center Point
Large Print

Also by William Heuman and available from Center Point Large Print:

Guns at Broken Bow
On to Santa Fe
Then Came Mulvane
Gunhand from Texas
Bullets for Mulvane
Roll the Wagons
Hunt the Man Down

HARDCASE HALLORAN

WILLIAM HEUMAN

CENTER POINT LARGE PRINT
THORNDIKE, MAINE

This Center Point Large Print edition
is published in the year 2024 by arrangement with
Golden West Inc.

Originally published in the US by Ace Books.

The text of this Large Print edition is unabridged.
In other aspects, this book may vary
from the original edition.
Printed in the United States of America
on permanent paper sourced using
environmentally responsible foresting methods.
Set in 16-point Times New Roman type.

ISBN 979-8-89164-245-4 (hardcover)
ISBN 979-8-89164-249-2 (paperback)

The Library of Congress has cataloged this record
under Library of Congress Control Number: 2024935908

CAST OF CHARACTERS

Thorpe Halloran
He'd come a thousand miles to clear his brother's name, but found it was much easier to ride into trouble than out of it.

Major Duveen
Rumor had it that he carried the whereabouts of a fortune in his head and the blood of many men on his hands.

Lauren Duveen
Blonde, beautiful, and high-spirited, the major's wife liked men and lost no time in telling Thorpe so.

Nate Welch
He was a coward hiding behind a big gun, and that made him all the more dangerous.

Durango
His was the fastest gun in the country, and before the fight was over, it would point to Thorpe.

Hallie Grant
This dark-haired beauty told Halloran that she wanted to see him back—alive.

I

The way Thorpe Halloran had it figured out, a man was going to die this night. He'd watched the little gunman come into the Alhambra Saloon and take his place at the bar a few yards away. Thorpe had labeled the man immediately, having seen this type too many times during the past half-dozen years.

The gunman had blond hair, a blond mustache, and very blue eyes. His hands were small and uncalloused, the hands of a man who lived by something other than hard labor. There was a tell-tale bulge under his black frock coat.

Leisurely, Thorpe sipped his beer and stared at his reflection in the bar mirror. He was tall, wiry, with tawny hair and gray eyes. There was a dent in his nose where a horse had kicked him when he was fourteen years old.

Like the little gunman at the bar with him, he also lived by the gun, but not in the same sense. He'd been a lawman on occasion; and then on other occasions when the law wasn't what it should have been, he'd been on the other side. Then he'd worked as a *pistolero* for a Mexican general south of the border, a general who'd been assassinated exactly eight days after Thorpe left his employ. He'd left it when he'd heard about the business with young Tom, his brother.

The woman who apparently owned this place came by, walking easily. She was dark-haired and brown-eyed and wore a black dress with little ornamentation. She had a straight way of looking at a man and she looked Thorpe in the eyes as she stopped to speak.

"Enjoying yourself?" she asked.

"Aim to," Thorpe said.

"Staying in town long?" she said.

"Long as I need for my business," Thorpe said.

A faint smile slid across the woman's face. She was not beautiful but she had looks, a good mouth and a straight nose. Her eyes were large, clear and unwavering. He figured her to be in her late twenties, a few years younger than himself. She had a full, rich figure. This was not a slip of a girl, but a mature woman.

Nodding toward the glass on the bar in front of Thorpe, she said, "This one is on the house. Enjoy yourself."

"Obliged." Thorpe nodded and watched her walk on past the blond-haired gunman at the bar.

He'd heard a man refer to her as Hallie. There had been no rings on her fingers; neither a wedding ring, nor rings for adornment, and Thorpe Halloran found himself wondering about this.

When the bartender went by, pausing to see

if Thorpe wanted anything, Thorpe said idly, “Hallie run this place?”

“Hallie Grant,” the bartender told him. “Joe Grant’s girl. Joe came here with the first stage coach goin’ through.”

Thorpe nodded. That explained her presence but it didn’t explain why she hadn’t found a man.

The blond gunman at the bar had had one drink and he’d gulped it down fast. He pushed the bottle away, indicating that one drink was all he would be having this night. This, too, was a sign that he was on the prod. A man about to go into action might take one stiff drink to steady himself, but the second or third would make him too confident or take the edge off his reflexes.

He turned at the bar, leaning back against it now and looking back at the crowd. This midweek night the saloon was fairly well-crowded. Almost all the card tables were occupied and more games were going on in the upstairs room.

Thorpe watched Hallie stop to chat with some of the men at a nearby card table, and then she signaled to one of her three bartenders to bring up a bottle.

The blond gunman glanced at Thorpe, his intense blue eyes flicking immediately to the Colt .44 on Thorpe’s hip, and that was another sign. His kind looked at a man’s gun even before he looked at the face.

Again Thorpe found himself wondering who

his victim was to be. He still hadn't made up his mind as to whether the blond man was the kind who put a bullet in another man's back or stood up to him straight and took his chances.

Finishing his drink, Thorpe moved across the room to an empty seat at one of the card games. He paused behind the chair, looking expectantly at the three men in the game.

One of the players said gruffly, "Sit down, friend."

Thorpe took his seat, pushed his hat back on his head, and signaled for a waiter to bring him chips. He was still watching the short blond man at the bar, though, as he was dealt his first hand. He was, therefore, immediately aware of it when the gunman's intended victim came into the saloon.

The little gunman stiffened when a stocky, barrel-chested man pushed in through the bat-wing doors, glanced over the room, and then headed toward the far end of the bar. He walked stiffly with his shoulders erect. Watching him, Thorpe was convinced that the man had had a military background. He had a solid jaw and a wide, unsmiling mouth.

He was dressed like one of the ranchers in the area, black, flat-crowned hat, dark coat, and string tie. There was a diamond ring on his finger, and the diamond flashed as his hand moved.

The blond fellow's blue eyes followed the

stocky man every moment until he reached the bar. Then the gunman pushed away from the bar, headed toward the door, and disappeared into the night.

Over the top of his cards Thorpe watched the stocky man at the bar, a slight frown coming to his face. As he tossed in three cards and waited for more to be dealt to him, he said to the dealer, "Figure I might know that chap at the end of the bar. You know his name, friend?"

He nodded toward the stocky man.

The card player grimaced and said, "Major Bennett Duveen. Runs D-Bar."

Thorpe nodded, his face expressionless. He'd come a thousand miles to see ex-Major Bennett Duveen, formerly attached to the Fifth Cavalry at Fort Landers, a hundred miles to the north. The very night that he'd arrived, a professional killer was preparing to set up Major Duveen.

Thorpe sat at the table, looking at his cards, not seeing them now as he thought of young Tom Halloran, his brother, dead almost a year. Tom had come out of West Point as a second lieutenant a year after Custer's defeat on the Little Big Horn. He'd been assigned for duty at Fort Landers, Dakota Territory. He'd been there only six months when the paymaster's wagon, containing the biggest payroll in the history of the Western Department had been hit by Indians and the entire escort of sixteen men had been wiped out—including Second Lieutenant Tom Halloran, in charge of the detail.

There had been some rumors that the "Indians" had not really been Indians. The quarter million dollars had disappeared completely even though Indians had no use for greenbacks, and at the Custer massacre greenbacks taken from dead troopers had been scattered over the plains like so much confetti.

The rumors circulating through this part of the country had been to the effect that white men had planned the raid and that Tom Halloran had deliberately led his escort into the trap and then had been double-crossed by his partners and killed.

Also, there were the rumors that a Major Duveen had resigned from the service and bought an immense ranch on the Powder River, thereafter setting himself up as a cattle baron. The rumors also had it that ex-Major Duveen, because of his suddenly acquired wealth, could know something about the paymaster's robbery.

Across the border Thorpe had heard these stories, coming in with hardcase riders who worked both sides of the Rio Grande, and he'd ridden north immediately to learn more.

In Benton he'd already discovered that Major Duveen was hiring guns on his payroll even though there was no range war pending and rustling here was no worse than anywhere else.

Sitting at the card table, Thorpe Halloran found himself wondering what had happened to the quarter million dollars. How had Major Duveen been able to purchase the largest ranch on the Powder River? Why was he now hiring guns?

The man at Thorpe's left said peevishly, "You in this pot, Jack?"

Thorpe looked at his cards and then tossed them in.

The card player, a scrawny, thin-faced man with a hatchet chin, had been having a run of bad luck, and he said irritably, "Man wants to play cards should play cards."

Thorpe sat back in the chair, his face expressionless. He said softly, "Somebody ask you, friend?"

The man with the hatchet chin looked at him and then dropped his eyes quickly. He opened his mouth as if to say something, but then changed his mind.

Thorpe watched as Major Duveen gulped his drink and then turned to look over the crowd. The major's wide, heavy-jawed face betrayed no emotion. His eyes were black, piercing, constantly moving.

Hallie Grant went by, had a word with Duveen, and then kept going. Thorpe found himself wondering whether there was anything between these two.

There were several empty chairs at card tables nearby, and had the major desired he could have sat in at the games, but he remained at the bar, still looking over the room as if watching for someone. Once his dark eyes came to rest on Thorpe and remained there for several moments.

Thorpe glanced at him coolly and then went back to his cards. If it was true that there were hardcases gunning for Bennett Duveen, then it was obvious that Duveen was trying to spot possible *pistoleros.*

A big, red-faced, light-haired fellow in his late thirties—perhaps a few years younger than Duveen—came into the saloon and moved up to where the major stood.

Without a word Duveen pushed the bottle toward him, and the bartender placed a shot glass in front of the red-faced man. The big fellow had a loose-jointed way of walking and his left shoulder seemed to be lower than the right. He had big, spade-like hands.

The red-faced man didn't say anything until he'd finished his drink and then he turned, put both elbows on the wood, and let his eyes move over the room.

Duveen said something to him, and he nodded without replying. Like Duveen, the big fellow's eyes also paused on Thorpe.

In this town strangers were immediately suspect.

Thorpe played another hand, yawned, then threw in his cards and stood up. He'd won a few dollars in the short time that he'd played. As he walked toward the bar now to cash his chips, he noticed that the big, red-faced man was watching him.

Pulling up a half-dozen feet from where the two men stood, Thorpe waited for the bartender to come toward him. In the bar mirror he saw the big fellow say something to Duveen, and then the major glanced his way, also.

Thorpe turned his head away to conceal the faint smile which crossed his face. They'd spotted him definitely as a stranger and it was quite obvious that ex-Major Bennett Duveen of the Fifth Cavalry did not relish strangers in Benton.

The bartender cashed the chips and Thorpe pointed to a bottle on the shelf. He was pouring himself a drink when the red-faced man moved over toward him. He was wearing a Colt .45 on his left hip.

"New in town?" the red-faced man asked, as he looked at Thorpe in the mirror.

Thorpe nodded.

"Stayin' long?" the red-faced man said.

Thorpe looked at him. "Everybody asks that same damn question," he observed.

"Everybody's not me," the big fellow told him flatly.

"Who the hell are you?" Thorpe said.

The big man blinked and his round jaw tightened. "Nate Welch," he said.

When Thorpe just shrugged and said nothing, Welch said, "I didn't hear your name, Jack."

Thorpe thought for a moment and then said casually, "Coleman."

"Stayin' in town?" Welch asked.

Thorpe turned to look at him. "You said that before," he said.

"An' you didn't answer."

"You the law in this town?"

Welch shook his head.

"Then go to hell," Thorpe said pleasantly.

He paid for his drink and he waited for Nate Welch to make something of this. Welch didn't want any more of it, though, and Thorpe knew his man now beyond any shadow of doubt. Welch was big and he carried a big gun, but it didn't mean anything.

Duveen came up then, touched Welch on the arm, and walked toward the door.

"Reckon you better learn to be more polite, mister, if you want to stay in this town," Welch growled before he left. He followed Duveen out through the bat-wing doors.

Thorpe turned to the bartender. "Welch ramrod for Major Duveen?" he asked.

The bartender nodded.

Behind him, Thorpe heard Hallie Grant say

quietly, “I wouldn’t tangle with them if I were you, mister.”

Thorpe turned to smile at her. “Who am I?” he countered.

Hallie looked him over thoughtfully and then nodded. “You’re tough,” she said, “but you’re only one. Remember that.”

“Always been enough before,” Thorpe said.

“You’ve never been here before,” Hallie said, and then she added thoughtfully, “You remind me of somebody.”

Thorpe wondered if Tom Halloran had been down this way on occasional furloughs. It would not have been unusual for Tom to spend a few days in Benton, the largest town near the post.

“I’m new here,” Thorpe told her.

Hallie smiled faintly. “Stay new,” she said, “and alive.”

II

Change jingling in his pocket, Thorpe walked toward the door of the saloon, the thought occurring to him that the little gunman who'd been waiting for Duveen might be biting off more than he could chew. Hallie Grant would know how tough Duveen's crew was.

Standing out on the walk, Thorpe saw the buckboard tied a short distance away with Nate Welch sitting up on the seat. Duveen was walking across the road toward a lighted store front which sported a gold-lettered sign: "Harrigan & Sloane, Attorneys at Law."

Benton was not too big a town, not as big as some Thorpe had been in, and it seemed reasonably quiet this evening. Along the main street a bank, two hotels, a Wells-Fargo office, a jailhouse, and several merchant shops.

Approaching it at mid-afternoon that day, he had reflected that it was an ideal place for a man to hole up if he had something to hide and wanted to live without attracting too much attention.

Standing out on the walk, Thorpe rolled himself a smoke as he watched Duveen step into the law office. He knew then that the little blond gunman who'd stood at the bar was not going to bring it out into the open, and he had contempt for the man.

Tossing away the match, Thorpe now turned left, walking past the buckboard where Welch sat, noticing as he did so that Welch was watching him carefully, the barrel of a shotgun protruding above the seat where he sat. He headed up toward the Benton House where he'd taken a room.

As he went up the walk a drunk weaved toward him and he maneuvered his way around the man. When he glanced back he noticed that Welch was still watching him from the buckboard.

As he entered the hotel and crossed the lobby, the desk clerk, a young man, prematurely bald, nodded to him. Thorpe nodded, smiled, and walked on toward the empty dining room. The clerk watched him in surprise because it was past ten o'clock and the dining room was closed.

Walking rapidly now, Thorpe crossed the dining room and stepped into the kitchen where a man was washing pots and pans. He nodded pleasantly to the man and stepped toward a door which opened on the rear of the hotel.

Outside, he paused, letting his eyes become accustomed to the darkness. Finishing the cigarette, he started walking quietly back toward the alley in which the little gunman was lying in wait for Major Duveen. He owed Duveen nothing, and Duveen did not even know him, but he did not intend to see the major shot down before he got to know a lot more about the man.

Passing at the rear of one of the saloons along

the street, he could hear the tinkle of a piano.

Thorpe stepped over a broken-down fence, making sure as he walked that he did not kick an empty tin can or stumble over any rubbish.

He paused at the head of the alley which was about eight feet across. He estimated the distance to the street as about forty feet. Through the thin wall of the building where he waited he could hear a man cursing stupidly, incessantly. At the far end of town a gun went off, and a cowboy whooped.

Crouching down, Thorpe removed his hat and then peered around the corner of the building. He could see a man down near the mouth of the alley, standing against the wall and clearly outlined against the light from the street. He could also see the horses harnessed to Duveen's buckboard where Nate Welch sat with the shotgun.

That shotgun wasn't going to be of any use, though, once the small man in the alley opened up with his pistol at a distance of ten feet when Duveen came out of the law office.

Putting his hat back on his head, Thorpe suddenly crawled into the alley and sat back against the wall motionless. While he could see the little gunman quite plainly, he was quite sure the gunman couldn't see him.

Now he began a slow approach toward his man, feeling carefully with his hands on the ground as he crawled forward and moving inches at a time.

It took him ten minutes to get half way down the alley, and then he stopped to sit back against the wall again, his gun across his knee. He waited.

It was fully thirty minutes before Duveen came out of the law office. Thorpe heard the door open and close on the street. He sat up now, holding the Colt gun steady and lowering his body closer to the ground.

The little fellow was standing close to the wall as he waited for Duveen to come into view, and then Thorpe called softly, "Back this way first, Jack."

He expected a shot and he was not disappointed. Any man who threw lead from an alley would shoot first and ask questions later. The gunman swung around and orange flame darted from the muzzle of his gun. The lead bounced off the brick wall of the building against which Thorpe was now leaning.

Thorpe's gun bucked in his hand. His bullet struck the little fellow, but he never learned whether the shot was deadly or not. The gunman was knocked out of the alley by the impact of the bullet. As he staggered out into the patch of light from the law office window, Nate Welch's shotgun boomed twice. The first load smashed him against the corner of the building; the second propelled him a half-dozen feet back into the alley.

Thorpe stood up, the gun in his hand, waiting.

He saw Duveen come into the patch of light, and then Nate Welch came running up, still carrying the shotgun.

“Who the hell’s in there?” Welch snapped.

“Hold your fire,” Thorpe said easily, and he walked forward, holstering his gun as he stepped out into the street.

Duveen stared at him and said nothing. Nate Welch said gruffly, “His bullet got him first, major.”

Bennett Duveen was inches shorter than Thorpe and he stared up at Thorpe thoughtfully.

“What were you doing in that alley?” he asked.

“Saving your life,” Thorpe said. “Saw this hombre come into the alley an’ I figured I knew what he had in mind.”

“You know him?” Duveen asked. He had a heavy voice, the voice of authority.

Thorpe shook his head. The crowd was beginning to gather, looking curiously into the alley.

“I don’t know him,” Thorpe said.

“You know me?” Duveen asked.

Again Thorpe shook his head.

“Why?” Duveen wanted to know.

“Reckon I don’t like to see a man shot from an alley,” Thorpe observed.

A tall, lantern-jawed man with a star on his vest pushed through the crowd, knelt down beside the dead man and struck a match. He came out of the alley in a few moments and he said to Major

Duveen, "Shotgun blasts." He looked at the greener in Welch's hands.

"Man tried to shoot me," Duveen told him quietly. "Nate, here, got him with the shotgun."

"That fellow hit him first," Welch said, nodding toward Thorpe.

The sheriff of Renton looked at Thorpe. "New in this town?" he asked, and Thorpe nodded. "Know the dead man?" the sheriff went on.

"Saw him in the Alhambra," Thorpe said. "Figured he was on the prod for someone. Turned out to be Major Duveen."

Across the road he saw Hallie Grant watching from in front of the Alhambra.

The sheriff said quietly, "My name's Ben Horner. Reckon you don't know why this hombre wanted to kill the major?"

Thorpe shook his head. "Rode in this afternoon," he said. "That's my part in it, sheriff."

Horner just scratched his long jaw and turned away. Major Duveen touched Thorpe's arm and said, "Would you mind stepping over to the buckboard for a moment."

He walked off with Nate Welch following him. Welch glanced back at Thorpe curiously as if trying to figure him out.

Thorpe walked to the rear of the buckboard where Duveen waited and he said, "All right."

"Your name's Coleman?" Major Duveen asked and Thorpe nodded.

"Looking for work?"

Thorpe smiled. "Could be," he said.

"I'm obliged to you for saving my life," Major Duveen told him. "If you're looking for a job, ride out to D-Bar tomorrow morning. I'm signing on riders."

"Reckon I'm not a rider," Thorpe observed, "if you mean punching cows."

"That wouldn't be your job," Duveen told him. "I want you around to do what you did tonight. The pay is two hundred a month. You stay in the bunkhouse with my riders."

Thorpe looked at him. "That's top money," he said.

Nate Welch said sourly, "You want it or not, Jack?"

"I'll take it," Thorpe said.

He stood on the walk and he watched Duveen and Nate Welch drive off in the buckboard. As he was standing there, Ben Horner came over and said to him, "I'd be careful, mister. That fellow you shot might have friends."

"They won't do him a damn bit of good now," Thorpe smiled, "but I'm obliged for the warning, sheriff."

He turned toward the hotel and as he walked he was thinking how easy it had been. He'd come to this town to learn more about Bennett Duveen and now he was working with Duveen. The rumors had been correct that Duveen, afraid of his life, was hiring guns for protection. He wondered what ex-Major Duveen would think if he knew that the last gun he'd hired might destroy him—if it proved true that Duveen *was* involved in the army payroll raid.

Thorpe had his black gelding in the hotel livery stable, and the next morning he saddled the animal and rode out of town. He passed Hallie Grant on the street, and she looked different in the morning. She was hatless; her dark hair shining in the bright sunlight.

Riding past her, Thorpe touched his hat. She smiled and nodded.

"I hear you've signed on with Duveen," she said, as Thorpe slowed down near her.

"Pay is good," Thorpe told her, "an' the work is easy. What's Duveen afraid of?"

Hallie Grant looked at Thorpe steadily. "Ask him," she said.

"Might do that," Thorpe smiled. He touched his hat again and rode on, leaving town.

This was range country with the grass hock high—a hilly country broken occasionally with small stands of timber. A thin line of willows twisting between the hills indicated the course of the river.

Thorpe had obtained the location of D-Bar from the desk clerk. He rode due west now, crossing the Powder, and climbing the low ridges, keeping to the stage road which went on to Sherman City.

A few miles out of town he hit the wagon trace which ran due south toward the D-Bar ranch, and immediately he spotted cattle carrying the D-Bar brand.

A rider went by with a dozen head and looked at Thorpe suspiciously. Thorpe forded a pebbly stream, a tributary of the Powder. The gelding was coming up out of the water when Thorpe heard a woman scream off toward his left at a distance of not more than a hundred feet.

Jerking the black around, he rode hard toward a clump of willows along the edge of the stream. When he smashed through the willow screen he saw a girl, in fawn-colored riding pants and white blouse, astride a dapple-gray horse.

Two men were on the ground nearby, one of them holding the gray's head, while the other man was trying to pull the girl from the saddle. The fellow holding the horse was a 'breed with jet black hair underneath his broken hat. He was a tall, rather thin fellow with a very dark complexion and high cheekbones.

The second man was a slovenly, bewhiskered fellow with a splotched, reddish face. He was trying to pull the girl from the saddle. She'd gotten one boot loose from the stirrup, and was kicking at him desperately.

The girl's hair was golden-blond, and she had

the most beautiful face Thorpe had ever seen: a full, rich mouth, perfectly shaped nose, and clear and slightly tanned skin.

As Thorpe broke into the clearing, the white man with the whiskers swung around. He wore a battered derby hat, a seedy black coat, and broken-down boots. He wasn't armed, but there was a rifle in the saddle holster on one of the two horses tied nearby.

The bewhiskered white man had close-set, bleary eyes and a blue-veined, bulbous nose. He stared at Thorpe grimly as he rubbed his hands on the sides of his pants.

Thorpe walked up and said softly, "You after the horse or the lady, mister?"

The bewhiskered man glanced back at the 'breed behind him. He said sourly, "None o' your damn business, Jack."

"Reckon it is," Thorpe told him, and then when he was within range, his right hand moved very fast, lifting the gun from the holster. He smashed the barrel across the man's brown derby hat.

As the bewhiskered fellow collapsed to his knees with a moan, Thorpe kicked out with his right boot, catching him full on the jaw and propelling him a half-dozen feet away.

He was ready when the 'breed leaped for him, knife in hand, lips drawn back in a snarl. Again the gun flashed, the barrel this time smashing across the 'breed's knife hand. There was a snap as the wrist broke and the 'breed fell to his knees, holding the hand.

Picking up the knife, Thorpe threw it into the stream. He said tensely, "You speak English?"

The 'breed stared up at him. He had a thin slit of a mouth with a broken tooth up front. When he nodded, Thorpe said to him, "When your friend comes to, you clear out. If I find you within a hundred miles of this spot by the morrow, you'll both be dead. *Savvy*?"

The 'breed nodded. Holding his broken wrist, he got to his feet and he walked back toward the horses, leaving the bewhiskered man still unconscious on the ground.

Thorpe called after him, "You pull that rifle out of the holster and you're dead."

He turned to the girl who was watching and he said, "Reckon you'd better ride out of here, ma'am. This place has a smell to it."

Her hat, a flat-crowned sombrero, had fallen to the ground and Thorpe picked it up. As he handed it to her, he noticed that her eyes were green and cool, the greenest eyes he'd ever seen in a woman.

"I'm obliged to you," she said. "This has never happened to me before, riding out alone."

"Riding far?" Thorpe asked.

"D-Bar," the girl said, and Thorpe stared at her. He figured she could have been in her early twenties, not too old to be Bennett Duveen's daughter, but then he saw the wedding ring on her finger.

"I'm Lauren Duveen," she said. There was the sleekness of the leopard about her and she'd quite recovered now from the ordeal. "My husband will send riders after those two if he finds out," she said.

Thorpe shrugged. "His business," he said. "Reckon I'm headin' toward D-Bar. I'll ride with you, Mrs. Duveen."

She glanced at him with warmth in her eyes. "Looking for the major?" she asked.

"Signed on last night," Thorpe said. It was the first intimation he'd had that Major Duveen was a married man. For some reason it had not occurred to him that Duveen would be married.

"Been out here long?" he asked.

"We were married eight months ago," Lauren Duveen told him. "I suppose I should know better than to ride too far from the ranch."

Thorpe thought about this. Duveen had married after resigning from the service.

"Do you know my husband?" Lauren asked as they rode along.

"Met him last night," Thorpe said—and he wondered how well she knew the ex-cavalry officer.

Topping a rise they came in sight of D-Bar. There was a cluster of buildings, some of log structure. The main house was a sawed-wood building, with a veranda extending across the entire front. The bunkhouse nearby was large enough to accommodate at least a dozen riders.

There were stables, two large corrals for breaking and branding, and then a smaller building near the main stable which could have been a second bunkhouse. All of it was located on a big bend of the Powder River.

As they moved their horses down the grade toward the ranch house, two D-Bar riders, swinging in from the right, stared at them. They were hard-faced men, both of them armed.

Bennett Duveen, himself, was waiting for them near the large corral as they crossed a meadow. Lauren said in a low voice to Thorpe, "I'm not going to tell him about those two animals. They've been punished, already."

Thorpe nodded and said nothing. He saw Nate Welch come out of the stable and join Major Duveen.

"I met your new rider on the way in," Lauren said as she stepped from the saddle.

"You didn't waste any time," Major Duveen said to Thorpe quietly. Thorpe wondered whether he was referring to his coming out to D-Bar quickly, or becoming acquainted with Lauren.

"Figured I'd start earning my pay," Thorpe told him.

Major Duveen glanced at his beautiful wife and

he said quietly, "Nate, here, will show you where to bunk."

Thorpe touched his hat to Lauren Duveen, received a warm smile in return, and then walked off, following Welch. The D-Bar ramrod said over his shoulder as he walked, "A smart man will stay away from the major's wife, mister."

Thorpe smiled and said nothing.

"You hear me?" Welch asked tersely.

"Reckon I heard you," Thorpe told him, "and to hell with you."

Welch turned to stare at him. "What you need, Jack," he said softly, "is to be cut down to size."

"Any time you'd like to try it," Thorpe observed, "reckon I'll be around."

"Somebody in this crew might just like to try it with you," Welch said, grinning.

"But not you," Thorpe said and then smiled.

"When I'm ready," Welch said.

He led Thorpe toward the smaller of the two bunkhouses. Thorpe suspected that the larger building housed the regular D-Bar cowpunchers who handled Duveen's herds, and the smaller bunkhouse was reserved for the hardcase riders he'd been bringing in for other reasons.

"What's my job?" Thorpe asked as they came up to the bunkhouse.

Welch smiled coldly. "When the major wants a few men to ride with him," he said, "you ride." Then he looked down at the gun on Thorpe's hip and he added, "An' you know what that's for, too."

The bunkhouse was empty when he stepped inside, and Thorpe picked out one of the half-dozen bunks which apparently was unoccupied. He tossed his bedroll on it.

When he came outside he said to Welch, "How many men the major have in this bunkhouse?"

"Six with you," Welch said, "an' not a damn one of 'em ever branded a steer." He grinned and added coldly, "Figure that Jug Hansen will be throwin' his brand on somebody around here before long."

Thorpe sat down on the bench outside and rolled a cigarette. He watched Major Duveen and Lauren walking toward the house. Welch said thoughtfully, "I don't know how you two met, but it's too damned bad that you did."

"Why?" Thorpe asked him.

"She likes men," Welch observed.

Thorpe had already guessed that much and this accounted for Major Duveen's uneasiness. The major had married a girl much too young for himself and a girl, too, who had her weaknesses.

Welch walked off, and Thorpe finished his cigarette. He flipped the butt away and walked down toward the stable, leading the gelding.

There was a card game going on the sunny side of the stable with four men sitting cross-legged on the ground playing with a greasy deck of cards. One of the men was a curly-haired giant with an enormous battered nose. His hair was almost white in color. He had tremendous shoulders and huge hands, which, nevertheless, seemed to handle the deck of cards quite adeptly.

The four men looked up at Thorpe and then one of them, a short, squint-eyed fellow with a harelip, said sourly, “New man?”

Thorpe nodded. These were the hardcases who occupied the bunkhouse with him and whose only duty was to protect Bennett Duveen and to enforce his will.

“Name’s Baines,” the harelipped man said. “Sit in if you want, friend.”

There was no particular enthusiasm in his voice and no dislike, either. Thorpe sat down, noticing as he did so that the other three men were sizing him up carefully.

The big fellow shuffled the cards with his powerful fingers and said, “You ain’t told us your name, friend.”

“Coleman,” Thorpe said. “You’ll know me the next time.”

“Deal the cards, Jug,” little Baines growled.

Thorpe glanced at the big fellow, realizing that this was the man Nate Welch intended to set on him.

Jug said casually, “You the hombre shot up that fellow in the alley last night in Benton?”

"Welch did most of it with the greener," Thorpe said.

"Hear you're a rough one," Jug said.

"I don't like to be pushed," Thorpe told him.

Big Jug Hansen smiled at him as he dealt a hand. "Ain't always what a man likes," he observed. "Is it now?"

Thorpe said nothing. He played through several hands and as they were playing Welch came over to watch for a few minutes. The D-Bar ramrod leaned against the corner of the building, a sly grin on his face, and said to Thorpe, "Meet everybody?"

Thorpe nodded.

"A tough crew," Welch said.

Thorpe smiled. "Now it's tougher," he said, and he saw Baines glance at him.

The game broke up an hour later and the crew moved toward the bunkhouse for dinner. As they did so Thorpe saw Welch say a few words to Jug Hansen.

Both crews ate in the larger bunkhouse and it was evident that the regular riders for D-Bar were a little uneasy in the presence of the hardcases from the smaller bunkhouse.

There was little conversation in the room. The men wolfed down the food in silence and then washed it down with steaming cups of black coffee. Then they stepped outside immediately to roll cigarettes and smoke in silence.

Thorpe noticed that Jug Hansen had been the first one to leave the bunkhouse and he was not too surprised when, on stepping out into the open, he saw Jug come to the door of the smaller bunkhouse and toss a bedroll and saddlebag out onto the ground.

One of the hardcases, a short stubby man by the name of Red Bannion, lit up a cigarette, and said to Thorpe, "Reckon that's your gear, friend."

Thorpe nodded. He rolled a cigarette and put a match to it.

Bannion had a flattened bulldog face and tough blue eyes. He said thoughtfully, "Reckon I'd let it ride. That damned Hansen can kill a man with his bare hands."

Thorpe shook out the match and threw it away. "Reckon he can," he said.

"Welch put Jug up to it," Bannion observed.

"Reckon so," Thorpe nodded, and then he started to walk toward the bunkhouse.

Leo Baines said to him as he went by, "Let him have his fun."

"Like hell," Thorpe said.

III

Jug Hansen had strolled down to the far corner of the bunkhouse and was standing there now, a cigar in his mouth, with the tip jutting toward the sky.

Without looking at him, Thorpe bent down and picked up his bedroll and saddlebag. He was whistling tunelessly as he walked back into the bunkhouse with his gear.

Hansen watched him, a contemptuous grin on his wide face.

The bunkhouse was empty and Thorpe walked over to the bunk where he'd dropped his gear that morning. Another bedroll lay on the bunk.

Dropping his own bedroll back on the bunk, he picked up the new one, and walking to the door with it, threw it out onto the hard-packed dirt in front of the bunkhouse.

Red Bannion and Leo Baines were watching him and he saw Bannion's eyebrows lift slightly. Nate Welch was watching down near the corral and Thorpe saw him move toward the bunkhouse his face creased in a grin.

Without even looking in Jug Hansen's direction, Thorpe sat down on the bench outside, still puffing on his cigarette. He heard Hansen's boots crunching the ground as the big man walked toward the door.

Without speaking, Hansen picked up his bedroll and walked back into the bunkhouse with it. As he did so, Thorpe stood up and moved toward the door. He watched Hansen cross the room to the bunk, drop his own bedroll on it, and then pick up Thorpe's.

Thorpe said casually, "I'd leave it there, friend."

Jug Hansen turned and looked at him. "Would you?" he asked.

Thorpe nodded.

Hansen walked toward the door, leaving the bedroll on the bunk. Thorpe stepped to one side and let him come out. Hansen looked at him and then took the cigar from his mouth and tapped the burning tip against the wall to put it out. Then he placed the cigar carefully on the edge of the bench nearby, evidently with the intention of relighting it a short while later. He said softly, "You're a tough one, mister, but I'm usin' that bunk tonight."

Thorpe shook his head. "Not tonight," he said. "Not ever."

Nate Welch had reached the bunkhouse and was standing a half-dozen yards away, smoking his cigar with relish, and watching them. The other D-Bar riders, having heard that a fight was brewing, were moving toward the smaller bunkhouse.

Beyond Nate Welch, Thorpe saw Major Duveen and Lauren coming out through the ranch house door. Duveen looked in their direction, and then he, too, moved toward them, Lauren coming on behind more slowly. She carried a riding quirt which she slapped gently against her leg as she walked.

Jug was saying, "You like to take off that gunbelt, mister?"

Thorpe nodded and began to unbuckle the belt. He was whistling again as he walked toward the bench with it. When he placed the belt on the bench he did it roughly, and the cigar Hansen had placed there dropped into the dust.

Thorpe took off his hat and placed it on the bench next to the gunbelt. As he turned and walked away from the bench he noticed that Major Duveen and Lauren had reached the circle of silent, watching men.

Hansen took off his hat and dropped it on the bench. He was shaking his head in admiration as he did so, and he said, "Damn, but you're a cool one."

He had enormous arms rippling with muscle. The wrists were thick, and powerful. He moved away from the bunkhouse now and he stood, hands on hips and feet spread slightly. He was well over six feet tall and he weighed at least half-a-hundred pounds more than Thorpe.

Thorpe watched him thoughtfully. There was one way to fight a man like this and that was to get to him fast and hard, and at the same time keep away from him. He realized that if Hansen once got those powerful arms around him he'd be finished.

Stopping six feet away, Thorpe said easily, "Come and get it, Jug."

Hansen grinned and took one step forward, and then Thorpe leaped at him, lashing out savagely with his right fist, catching the surprised Jug on the side of the cheek and ripping the flesh.

The blood gushed from the deep gash on the cheekbone. As Hansen stepped back, Thorpe was on top of him like a cat, smashing punches into the giant's face, driving him back against the wall of the bunkhouse.

When the big fellow finally flung Thorpe off, his face was cut and bleeding from a half-dozen wounds. Blood dripped from his mouth, from his nose, from the corner of his right eye.

He wasn't finished, though. Driving in at Thorpe, he aimed a blow at Thorpe's body with his right hand, which if it had landed would have caved in Thorpe's ribs.

Thorpe pulled back in time, though, and as Hansen's fist grazed his rib, Thorpe swung hard with his left fist, catching Jug full in the mouth, loosening several teeth. This time Jug's knees buckled, but again he recovered and lunged in, trying to grab Thorpe around the waist.

As he came in, arms outstretched, figuring that Thorpe would try to back away from him, Thorpe stepped in. He began to rip punches up into Jug's stomach—hard, slogging, slashing punches, hitting with both fists, and as he struck he could feel the strength begin to leave the giant.

Jug's mouth opened wide in agony. He gasped and choked for air as he retreated, Thorpe pushing him back toward the wall of the bunkhouse. Suddenly, Thorpe stopped, pulled back, and then as Hansen slumped toward him, hands clasped across his stomach, Thorpe swung his right fist at the big fellow's jaw, getting all his weight behind it.

There was a sickening thud. Jug's head jerked around and he fell forward on his face and lay still. Thorpe took one look at him, realized that the fight was over, and then turned and walked down toward the horse trough near the corral. He washed the blood from his knuckles.

He passed Lauren Duveen on the way down, and he said softly as he went by, "Like it?"

Lauren just looked at him, her eyes narrowed. She hadn't flinched at the sight of the blood. As a matter of fact he was quite convinced that she'd enjoyed it.

He walked back toward the bunkhouse where Bannion and Baines had dragged the unconscious Hansen back to the bench and were sitting him up. Another man came up with a bucket of water and a towel and they began to wash the blood from Jug's battered face.

Thorpe was buckling on his gunbelt when Nate

Welch came up, puffing on the cigar. He looked at Jug critically and he said, “Didn’t figure you could do it.”

“Try it yourself next time,” Thorpe invited.

“I don’t have to fight you to prove anything,” Welch grinned.

“Maybe you do and maybe you don’t,” Thorpe told him, “but remember this, mister, don’t send any more.”

He walked into the bunkhouse then and picked up the gear on the bunk which he and Jug had been fighting over. He walked with his stuff to an empty bunk at the far end of the room, dropping it there and leaving Jug in possession of the original bunk.

When he went outside he noticed that the big fellow was now recovering consciousness. Bannion said, “You damn near killed this man.”

“He’s tough,” Thorpe observed.

Jug was looking at him with one eye, the other still closed. He shook his head and mumbled something which Thorpe could not catch.

Bannion said, “He says he ain’t sore at you.”

Thorpe smiled. “Nothing to be sore about,” he said, and he patted Jug’s shoulder.

Walking back into the bunkhouse he opened his saddlebag, took a cigar from the bag and went outside.

“Owe you this one, Jug,” he said. Then he walked on toward the stable, noticing as he did so that Major Duveen and his wife were standing out in front of the house, evidently having a few words. Lauren Duveen's body was tense as she stared at her husband whose back was toward Thorpe.

Very suddenly, Lauren turned away and walked toward the dapple-gray horse she'd been riding that morning when Thorpe had met her. Angrily, she stepped into the saddle, pulled the gray round, and rode away.

Duveen walked into the ranch house, his wide shoulders set stiff.

Saddling the gelding, Thorpe rode off, paralleling the direction taken by Lauren. It was quite evident that Major Duveen and his young wife were not the most happily-married couple in the territory. If there was anything he, Thorpe Halloran, wanted to learn about Bennett Duveen, perhaps the best source of information could be his wife.

Thorpe rode due south, watching Lauren disappear over a ridge a short distance away. It was about two o'clock in the afternoon now, and a hot sun blazed down upon the hills.

A mile south of the ranch he started to cut over in Lauren's direction and spotted the dapple gray just disappearing over another ridge. When she reached the bottom of the grade Thorpe moved his black down toward her and she pulled up, undoubtedly recognizing the horse.

"Ridin' again?" Thorpe smiled. "Figured you might have had enough this morning."

Lauren stared at him. "Did you follow me?" she asked.

Thorpe shrugged. "That could be," he admitted.

She started riding again and Thorpe moved the black gelding beside her. He could see that she was still quite agitated over the argument she'd had with her husband.

"Reckon the major's kind of on edge these days," Thorpe observed, watching her face as she rode. "Man tried to put a bullet in him last night from an alley, and from what I hear, it's happened before."

"It'll keep happening, too," Lauren scowled.

Thorpe rubbed his jaw. "Must be a hell of a lot of people want him dead," he observed. "He got that many enemies?"

"He has enemies," Lauren nodded. "That's why men like you were hired."

"If we knew who the enemies were," Thorpe observed, "reckon we can keep him alive longer."

Lauren shook her head. "I don't know who they are," she said, "and I don't know why they want him dead. I know he's been buying up a lot of range land around here and pushing some men pretty hard when they refuse to sell. Then he's driven some rustlers out of the country, too."

Thorpe nodded and he was quite sure that Lauren Duveen did not know about the army payroll raid or the fact that rumors had gone out that Major Duveen had nearly a quarter of a million dollars in greenbacks stashed away.

They rode on for another half-mile and then Lauren swung around and headed back. “I feel better now,” she said gratefully.

Thorpe only smiled.

“You’d better not ride back to the ranch with me,” Lauren told him. “The major doesn’t like me to be around other men.”

“I’ll move out,” he told her and he pulled the gelding away, riding back toward D-Bar from a different direction. He took his time coming back in, also, pausing to look in at an abandoned homestead, one which he had no doubt Duveen had bought to include as part of his huge range.

When he returned to the ranch late in the afternoon, Welch met him as he was dismounting outside the stable.

“Where the hell you been?” Welch snapped.

Thorpe looked at him. “No damn orders to stay here,” he observed.

“When there’s no orders you stick around,” Welch growled.

“Reckon, I’ll take orders from Duveen,” Thorpe said, “not you. I’m not one of your damned cowboys.”

Welch stared at him with hatred in his green eyes. “Duveen’s orders are to ride tonight,” he snapped. “You stick around, mister.”

Thorpe walked the gelding into the stable and threw down a few pitchforks of hay for the animal. When he came outside Leo Baines was waiting for him.

Hansen came up, his face bandaged, and he said, shaking his head, "You were a damned buzz saw, mister."

"Wouldn't like to try it again," Thorpe told him. He said to Baines, "What happens tonight? Hear we're riding."

Baines nodded.

"Where?" Thorpe asked.

Baines shrugged. "Just ridin'," he said. "When we git there, Duveen gives the orders. He's payin' the money."

Thorpe said carefully, "Reckon he's got a hell of a lot to pay out, too, hasn't he?"

Baines looked at him and then at Red Bannion nearby, but he only nodded, his expression blank.

He knows, Thorpe thought. *Bannion knows, too.*

IV

It was after dusk when they saddled up, the six riders from the small bunkhouse, along with Major Duveen and Nate Welch. From the stable Thorpe saw the yellow lamplight in the windows of the ranch house, and as they were about to ride away he saw Lauren Duveen come out onto the verandah.

There were no questions asked by any of the men. They sat astride their mounts, some of them smoking, waiting. Bennett Duveen sat upon a chestnut mare, a blocky figure of a man with square-set shoulders, thick neck, and heavy jaw.

Nat Welch adjusted the Colt gun on his hip and then looked back at the crew. His left shoulder drooped, making it seem as if his head was cocked to one side in an attitude of listening.

Duveen now swung the mare around and moved down past the corral and out across the meadow. Welch rode slightly behind him and the half-dozen hardcases followed in a straggly line. Thorpe brought up the rear with Jug Hansen just ahead of him, adhesive patches on his face, giving him a strange ghost-like appearance.

There was a half moon in the sky providing plenty of light, and they rode due west, moving up into the hills, and passing clumps of D-Bar stock bedded down for the night. Thorpe rolled a cigarette as he rocked gently in the saddle.

They forded a small stream, Major Duveen still riding at a leisurely pace, a cigar in his mouth now. After crossing the stream they began to swing toward the south and a short while later raised the lights of a small ranch.

When Duveen pulled up the chestnut, Thorpe realized that this was their destination. Down below in the ranch house lived a homesteader or small rancher, who probably had not accepted Bennett Duveen's offer to buy him out. Because of this, he had to be taught a lesson this night. Thorpe had seen it happen before and he'd never liked it. He wondered, though, how far Duveen would go with a stubborn rancher.

The major was having a few words with Nate Welch, and now Welch rode forward toward the house. When he'd gone about fifty yards Duveen turned and signaled for the riders behind him to come along. He rode on slowly behind Welch, pausing when they were twenty-five yards from the ranch house.

A dog had started to bark by now, and Thorpe saw a door open and a man come out and stand in a patch of yellow light. The house was very small, of logs, with several outbuildings nearby and a corral, which was empty.

In the shadows Thorpe now saw Nate Welch still astride his blue roan, talking with the man.

Duveen sat where he was, unmoving, the cigar butt glowing near his mouth.

Suddenly the rancher walked past Welch and came on toward the spot where the others were waiting, and as he walked Thorpe saw the bulge of a gun on his hip. The rancher had evidently strapped on a gun before coming out into the night.

Welch turned his horse and walked after him, making no attempt to stop the man. In the moonlight Thorpe could see the rancher quite clearly. He was tall, stringy, with a long jaw and straight black hair which seemed to be falling in his eyes.

"You ain't pushin' me out o' this country, major," the lank man said grimly. "I'm here to stay, same as you are."

"I've spoken to you before, Farnham," Major Duveen told him. "I won't come out again."

Farnham pulled back, his lower jaw sagging. "Who the hell you think you are, major?" he asked. "The Almighty, Himself? You can't tell a man to go an' he goes."

"I'm telling you," Duveen said steadily. "You're going tonight, Farnham, one way or the other."

Farnham stared at him and then at the semi-circle of silent men on horseback behind him. Thorpe sat astride the black gelding, shoulders hunched, the cigarette drooping in his mouth, a frown on his face. This was not new; he'd seen it happen before—the big man driving the small man out of the country.

Welch came riding up and he said soothingly, "Lem, don't be a damned fool. Just pack up your gear an' head out. You got money; you're gettin' paid for this place, an' there's only you to worry about."

"Me is enough," Farnham blurted out.

"You ain't got much choice," Welch observed. "Matter of fact you got five minutes, Lem."

"I ain't goin'," Lem told him grimly and he backed away a few steps.

"You do as I say," Major Duveen roared suddenly, and Thorpe stared at the short cavalryman in surprise. This was a new facet of the man. Duveen was a military commander giving an order and he wanted it obeyed. "You put out of here tonight, Farnham. You hear me?"

Lem Farnham's mouth was working. Thorpe watched the man and then his eyes moved toward Duveen and he wondered if the major would order them to shoot the man down. If that order came he knew that he, himself, would not obey it. There were eight men here against one.

"I ain't goin'," Lem Farnham said again, his voice low and tense.

"You hear me?" Major Duveen said, his voice dropping now so that Thorpe, sitting only ten feet away, could scarcely hear him.

Instead of replying Lem suddenly turned and

started to run, zig-zagging back toward the house.

"Lem!" Major Duveen roared and then he jerked his chestnut mare around. "Now!" he barked at the men with him.

The six hardcases behind him just looked. Only Nate Welch drew his gun.

"Now!" Bennett Duveen raged. "Now! Do you hear me!"

Welch hesitated and then sent one shot after the fleeing man, aiming high, Thorpe figured, to miss him. Lem pulled up, and as he swung he drew his gun and got off a shot. The lead went wild and Thorpe heard it sing over their heads.

"Now!" Major Duveen roared.

Nate Welch stared back at the six unmoving men behind him, and then raised his gun again, firing more carefully this time. Lem dropped to the ground, and from the way he fell Thorpe knew he was dead. It was as if all the bones had been taken out of Lem Farnham's body and he was jelly collapsing.

Welch holstered his gun, sent another injured look back at the hardcases, and then rode forward slowly, cursing as he did so. Duveen came on behind him, his big shoulders still set.

Leo Baines said, "Hell of a business."

Red Bannion said, "He figures he needed six guns on this sodbuster?"

Thorpe said nothing, but he hadn't liked the odds tonight. It had been little less than sheer murder out at this lonely ranch house. Duveen rode up slowly to where Nate Welch had dismounted and was holding a lighted match over Farnham's face.

"Dead as hell," Welch said. "Damn it! He shouldn't have pulled a gun on us." He glared at the six men sitting astride their horses as they moved up closer. "What the hell happened to you boys?" he grated. Thorpe could see that he was still a little shaken.

Thorpe spoke for all of them. He said softly, "What the hell did you want with us, Nate?"

Major Duveen said quietly, "He was a damned fool. He never should have drawn a gun."

In a sense it was true. Farnham shouldn't have drawn a gun with eight men in front of him. It was like a man trying to fill a flush by drawing four cards. It just hadn't made sense.

Welch said glumly, "What in hell we gonna do with him? We can't have Horner ridin' out here an' askin' questions."

Duveen dismounted and walked toward the log ranch house. He said over his shoulder to Welch, "Bring him into the house."

Welch straightened up, rubbed his hands on the sides of his pants, and said sullenly, "Give me a hand here somebody."

He bent down and lifted Farnham by the armpits, waiting for someone else to help him. He didn't lift Farnham any higher, though, because none of the hardcases had dismounted. They sat astride their horses looking down at him.

"All right!" Welch snapped. "All right. Give me a hand here. You, Baines."

Leo Baines sat where he was, making no move to dismount. With his harelip in the dim light, it looked as if he were grinning at Welch.

Thorpe said, a touch of humor in his voice, "Your bag, Welch. Reckon you're entitled to him."

Cursing, Nate Welch started to drag the dead man toward the house where Duveen was waiting for him.

Bannion said curiously, "What the hell they gonna do now?"

"I got an idea," Baines told him, and Thorpe had an idea, also, which was confirmed a short while later when they saw an unusual light in the windows—a light brighter than the lamp which had been burning before.

One of the hardcases, a fellow by the name of Dave Shaw, said, "They're burnin' the damn place down!"

Jug Hansen cursed as Duveen and Welch came out of the house alone and the flames began to lick toward the windows.

"They got no right—," Jug started to say, but Bannion said idly, "Man's dead, Jug. Ain't nothin' worse you can do to him than that."

Thorpe watched Duveen and Welch come

back toward them as the flames began to crackle inside the building. Duveen never even stopped to look back. He rode on past the six men, his flat-crowned hat pulled low over his eyes. He rode erect, shoulders back, right hand at his side.

Welch was still grumbling, and because he grumbled and because he cursed, Thorpe Halloran recognized him as a weak man, a man with a big gun—but still a weak man.

"What a hell of a crew," Welch was saying bitterly. "I don't know why you boys are drawin' big money."

"You tell us why," Red Bannion said, but Welch had no answer. He rode on after Duveen and the six men followed him, Hansen turning his head to look back at the leaping flames mounting into the air. The ranch house was now burning like tinder.

Thorpe said to Baines, "This happen before?"

"The last one run when he was told," Baines observed. "This one wouldn't."

"Duveen try to buy him out and he wouldn't sell?"

"Ask the major," Baines laughed mirthlessly. "That ain't my business, friend. We're paid to ride around an' look tough an' maybe be tough if things get bad for the major."

Bannion said, "Don't ask too many damned questions when the pay is good an' the work is easy. I've been here six weeks now an' that was the first time anybody threw lead near me."

When they were a quarter of a mile away from the burning ranch house Thorpe pulled up and looked back. The little house was now a mass of flames. He sat there, staring at it, watching the sparks fly toward the sky and he was thinking bitterly, Where had Major Bennett Duveen learned that trick? Had he practiced it first with the paymaster's wagon after taking a quarter million dollars from the strongbox and leaving sixteen United States troopers dead on the ground?

"Some day we'll know," Thorpe said softly.

He rode on and Red Bannion said as he came up, "You say something, Coleman?"

"Reckon it wasn't important," Thorpe said.

When they reached D-Bar, Duveen dismounted, gave Welch his horse, and strode toward the house.

Red Bannion said to Thorpe, "Orders are that two men have to be here all the time. Tonight Dave Shaw an' Jug are stayin'. Figure I can stand a drink in town."

He looked at Thorpe expectantly.

"Ride with you," Thorpe said.

Leo Baines said, "Have to get that damn smell o' burnin' flesh out o' my nose."

"You didn't smell it," Thorpe said. "We were too far away."

"I can smell it," Baines scowled. "Smelled it before."

The three of them rode off in the direction of town and as they rode Bannion said thoughtfully, "That Duveen's a damn cool one, though, ain't he?"

"When he wants a man dead," Thorpe said, "he wants him dead."

"An' who's the next one?" Bannion asked.

"Maybe Duveen, himself," Baines grinned. "Somebody near got him in town last night if our friend here hadn't spoiled it, an' there must be plenty more where he come from."

When they reached Benton it was past ten, and they stepped into the Alhambra Saloon. Hallie Grant was at the bar talking with Ben Horner as the three men came in. She looked at Thorpe and her dark eyes had an odd expression.

Thorpe nodded to her and pulled up at the bar, a few feet away. The bartender brought them a bottle and three shot glasses, and then Ben Horner turned around and said without any expression in his voice, "The man with the big gun."

"And still loaded," Thorpe said.

Horner looked at him. "Don't use it in this town," he warned, "unless you've got a pretty damned good reason."

"Never use a gun," Thorpe told him, "unless I have a damned good reason."

Horner frowned. "You ride for Duveen now?" he asked.

Thorpe nodded and Horner said glumly, "Man's

got enough guns out at D-Bar to start a small war."

"Maybe that's what he's starting," Thorpe said, "a war."

He had his drink and then Bannion and Baines sat in at a card game, Thorpe remaining at the bar. He was still standing there, nursing his drink, when Hallie Grant paused in front of him.

"I'd like a word with you," she said, "alone."

Thorpe looked at her and nodded briefly.

"My quarters are upstairs," she told him, "door on the left. Be there in ten minutes."

"You trust me?" Thorpe smiled.

Hallie smiled. "I trust you," she said and she walked off.

For a few minutes Thorpe looked in at a card game, standing with his back against the wall, and after a while he headed up the stairs.

There were several private gaming rooms on the second floor with the doors open, and he could look inside. In one smoke-filled room a card game was going on, five men at the table. From the pile of chips out in the center, he realized that this was one of the big games in Benton.

Moving on past this door he came to the door on the left, pausing here to knock. The door was opened immediately by Hallie.

"Come in," she said.

Thorpe walked into the room, noticing that it was quite tastefully furnished with heavy mohair furniture and a red carpet. The wooden corner cabinet gleamed with polish. A tasseled light hung over the table in the center of the room.

Thorpe stood with his hat in his hand. Hallie closed the door behind him and stood against it. Then she said quietly, "Lieutenant Tom Halloran."

Thorpe turned around. "You know him?" he asked after a pause.

Hallie nodded. "Lieutenant Halloran was in here a number of times and I have a good memory for faces. Now you're related, aren't you?"

"Brother," Thorpe nodded.

"Why are you in this town under an assumed name?" Hallie wanted to know. She still stood by the door, her arms folded, watching him.

Thorpe shrugged. "A few things I'd like to find out," he said.

"About Major Duveen?" Hallie asked him.

Thorpe looked at her. "That could be," he admitted.

Hallie sat down at the table and looked up at him. There was a shadow in her fine brown eyes.

"You'll be killed before you find out," she said.

"Find out what?" Thorpe asked.

"What you want to know."

Thorpe frowned. "What do you know about it?" he asked. "You've heard the rumors?"

"I've heard the rumors," Hallie admitted. "That's all I know."

Thorpe said slowly, "Man serves all of his life in the army at officer's pay and then he retires and buys the biggest ranch in this part of the country and sets himself up as top man. Not only that but he's been trying to buy out everybody else. Where the hell does the money come from?"

Hallie just looked at him.

"A quarter million dollars was in that paymaster's wagon," Thorpe went on tersely. "My brother was in charge. There have been some rotten stories going on about him."

"I met your brother," Hallie told him. "He wouldn't do such a thing."

"Who did?" Thorpe scowled. "Who killed sixteen troopers and walked off with two hundred and fifty thousand dollars in greenbacks."

"Maybe someday you'll find out," Hallie Grant said, "and then you'll be dead."

"I won't be dead alone," Thorpe grated.

"He could have been dead last night," Hallie observed, "if you'd wanted it that way."

"I have to know first," Thorpe said. "Now I'm only guessing. If he's dead I'll never know."

Hallie nodded. "That's why you signed on with his crew," she said. "Now you can watch him. You think he's papered the walls of his ranch with those greenbacks? You might never learn anything, anyway."

"I can try," Thorpe stated.

"You could try with his wife," Hallie observed. "She hates him."

Thorpe looked at her. "How do you know?" he asked, amused.

"A woman knows," Hallie smiled. "I've seen them together. She's a beautiful girl—or hadn't you noticed?"

"I noticed," Thorpe said soberly.

Hallie went out into a small kitchen and came back with coffee on a tray, placing a cup before him.

"You've come a long distance?" she asked.

"Across the border," Thorpe said. "That's how far these stories have gone." He paused and he said, "What about Welch?"

"What about Welch?" Hallie asked over her cup.

"They known each other a long time?" Thorpe asked. "They know each other before Major Duveen came out of the army?"

Hallie shook her head. "I wouldn't know about that," she said.

"And who was the little gunman tried to shoot him last night?" Thorpe asked.

Hallie sipped her coffee. "Could have been a lot of reasons for that," she said. "The major has made many enemies since coming to Benton. He's pushing people hard. They may have hired a professional gun, or it could have been out of revenge."

Thorpe looked down at his cup. “You knew my brother,” he said. “You know he wasn’t in this dirty business. I’m here to clear him.”

Hallie nodded. “If there’s anything I can do,” she promised, “I’ll do it. I hear things in the Alhambra. I meet people.”

“I’m obliged,” Thorpe said.

Hallie stood up. “Watch how you walk,” she warned. “If they find out why you’re here you won’t live long. I’ll be listening and if I hear anything you’ll hear about it, too.”

Thorpe finished his coffee, thanked her again, and got up. He said at the door, “Mrs. Duveen’s not the only beautiful woman in this town.”

There was a faint flush in Hallie’s cheeks as he went out. He stopped to watch a card game upstairs for a while, and then he came down to the bar.

It was well past midnight when the three men rode out of town, heading back toward D-Bar. As they were riding Baines said glumly, “Still got that damn smell in my nose.”

“He’s dead.” Bannion observed. “Ain’t no use cryin’ over a dead man.”

“Wasn’t no way to finish off a man,” Baines scowled, and Thorpe could see that he was still affected by the incident. “Every man should be buried decent.”

“You figure Duveen should have called in Horner?” Red Bannion grinned, “an’ asked him to say a few words after Welch put the bullet in that sodbuster? He was dead."

When they reached D-Bar, Thorpe noticed that some of the lights were on in the main house as they went by. Bannion noticed it, also, and he said reflectively, "Reckon the major an' his lady are havin' it out with each other again!"

Thorpe didn't say anything. All of his life Duveen had been accustomed to giving orders, and obviously Lauren did not like to obey them.

After seeing to their horses Thorpe made a smoke outside the bunkhouse door before turning in. He sat on the bench, his hat pulled low over his face, arms folded across his chest, watching the lights in the ranch house beyond the corral.

As he watched he heard a door slam and a moment later he saw Lauren, her white blouse ghostly in the dim light, striding past the corral toward the stable.

Throwing away the cigarette, he stood up. Walking down to the stable he could see Lauren inside saddling her dapple gray. She worked feverishly throwing her light English saddle across the horse's back and tightening the cinches.

As Thorpe crew closer, Lauren stepped into the saddle and rode out, not even seeing him in the shadows. He watched her go and then he walked into the stable and saddled the black. He rode after her, seeing her up ahead, her white blouse against the darkened landscape. She was riding fairly fast, heading in a westerly direction away from Benton.

He had no doubt now that she'd had words with the major and had taken off like this in a fine fury. He told himself, also, that he was a damn fool riding after her, but he kept going anyway.

V

About two miles from the ranch Lauren pulled up, stopping on a small knoll at the edge of a growth of timber. Thorpe kept riding and as he drew closer the girl called sharply, "Who is it?"

"Coleman," he said.

Lauren had dismounted. Thorpe rode up and stepped down out of the saddle.

"Are you following me again?" she asked, and she did not sound too displeased.

"Hell of a time to be riding around," Thorpe observed. "Figured I'd keep you in sight."

"You're quite concerned about me, aren't you?" Lauren asked.

"I could be," Thorpe said. "I work for your husband."

"That the only reason?" Lauren asked, and she stepped toward him.

He could see her face in the dim light.

"Why do you think I rode out here?" she asked softly.

Thorpe smiled. "Figured you'd had a little trouble with the major," he said. "You wanted to be alone."

"I'm not alone now," Lauren told him, and then she put her hands on his shoulders.

A thin smile on his face, Thorpe pulled her

closer and kissed her full on the mouth. He held her tight for a moment and then he released her.

"I didn't think you'd do it," Lauren whispered.

"Why not?" Thorpe asked.

"You're not afraid of the major, are you?"

He kissed her again and he said, "What do you think?"

"I don't think you're afraid of the devil, himself," Lauren chuckled, "and now I think we'd better get back to the ranch."

"You're saying it," Thorpe told her.

Lauren looked at him and then she nodded. "I'm saying it," she said, "but I'm glad you came out."

They rode back together and as they were riding Thorpe said casually, "Reckon the major has plenty of enemies in this part of the country. He have 'em when he was in the service, too?"

"I didn't know him when he was in the service," Lauren explained. "He came to Chicago for a short spell after retiring and we became acquainted through a mutual friend."

When they spotted the lights of the ranch house Lauren said, "I'd better ride in alone."

Thorpe just nodded. After she'd ridden off he circled and swung in behind the stable, dismounting in front of the open door. As he was walking the black inside he saw a cigarette butt glowing in the shadows to one side.

When he stopped, Nate Welch called out to him softly, “You’re ridin’ late, Coleman.”

Thorpe looked at him steadily. “When nobody needs me,” he said, “I ride when I damn please.”

“Reckon that goes who you ride with, too,” Welch said evenly. “That right?”

“You Duveen’s spy or ramrod?” Thorpe asked him.

Welch flipped his cigarette away. “That wouldn’t have to be any o’ your damn business now would it?” he asked and then walked off.

In the morning Thorpe was seated on top of the corral rail watching one of the hands break a horse when Major Duveen came out of the house and passed him on the way to the stable. The major nodded briefly and kept going. Thorpe was convinced that Welch had said nothing about the night ride. He wondered about this.

At eleven, Sheriff Ben Horner arrived. His face was grim. Thorpe heard him say to Nate Welch, “You boys hear your neighbor had a fire last night and was burned in it?”

Welch shrugged. “Man shouldn’t be so damned careless,” he said.

“Nobody see those flames in the sky?” Horner asked, looking around at the knot of silent men in front of the bunkhouse.

“Reckon nobody was looking, sheriff,” Welch told him.

Horner looked from one man to the other and then he moved on toward the ranch house. Thorpe saw him talking with Major Duveen minutes later.

When Horner eventually rode off, Bannion said, "He didn't learn a damn thing, but he knows an' everybody else knows that Farnham didn't set his own place on fire an' burn himself up."

Jug Hansen came out of the bunkhouse, his face still puffed and bruised, and, as he was lighting up a smoke, he said to Thorpe, "What in hell would happen if somebody told Horner, it was Welch threw that lead at the sodbuster?"

"He might be dead," Thorpe observed.

They had another card game that morning and when they were finishing up a rider spurred in from the south, had a quick conference with Nate Welch. Welch then strode toward the ranch house, a frown on his red face.

Thirty minutes later Welch came out of the ranch house and headed toward the bunkhouse. Thorpe had just finished dinner and had come out into the bright sunshine when Welch came over to him.

"Saddle up," the D-Bar ramrod said tersely. Then he stepped to the bunkhouse door and called in sharply. "Saddle up. Everybody saddle up."

Thorpe strolled down to the stable and he

was throwing his saddle on the black when Leo Baines came in. Baines said curiously, "What in hell's up?"

Dave Shaw, who had his sorrel horse in the stall next to Thorpe's black, said, "Reckon Welch has a devil after him. Man's worried stiff."

Thorpe had noticed that, too. Nate Welch did have a queer look in his green eyes—the look of fear.

The six riders sat astride their mounts put in front of the stable while Welch had another brief conference in the house. When he came out, Duveen was with him and the two men spoke for a few moments near the door before Welch walked down to mount his blue roan.

Leo Baines asked, "Where in hell we ridin', Nate?"

"Avalon," Welch growled. "You'll hear about it later."

Thorpe rode beside Leo Baines as they moved around the corral and headed south and west up into the hills. He said as they were riding, "Where's Avalon?"

"Seven—eight miles south an' west," Baines told him. "Ghost town. Wasn't a damn soul there last time I came through."

Thorpe glanced back at the four hardcase riders coming upon behind them and he said thoughtfully, "Reckon there's more than ghosts there now and it's got Welch worried."

Baines shrugged and grinned. “Reckon our job is to keep Duveen happy an’ alive. We can’t do that, he hires somebody else.”

They dipped down into a draw and came up on the other side, moving on again, always toward the south. Welch was still up ahead of them, riding silently, morosely, that one shoulder sagging.

A mile beyond the draw they hit timber with a stream running through it. Welch stopped here to let them water the horses, but Thorpe knew he had another reason for the halt.

Welch stood at the edge of the stream, digging at a stone with the tip of his boot, and then he said casually, “Might be a little trouble in Avalon.”

“Shouldn’t be,” Baines smiled. “Nobody there.”

“Bunch there now,” Welch observed. “Four of ’em. Chap by the name of Durango leadin’ ’em, an’ Durango’s tough.”

Red Bannion said, “Tough for who?”

Nate Welch just looked at him. “Durango’s here to make trouble for the major,” he said. “Reckon you boys know you’re hired to see that he don’t.”

“How many?” Dave Shaw asked.

“Four,” Welch said again.

Bannion said, “You askin’ us to ride in an’ shoot this bunch up, Nate?”

Welch shrugged. “Figure what to do when we get there. They either leave or they’ll be dead.”

“Like Farnham,” Leo Baines murmured.

Welch stared at him. “Farnham had a chance to get out,” he snapped.

Bannion said, “You figure they’ll open up on us when we ride in?”

“They won’t know who the hell we are right away,” Welch said.

“They know Duveen,” Thorpe said, his face expressionless.

Nate Welch looked at him. “They know the major,” he nodded.

“Man has a hell of a lot of people don’t like him,” Thorpe observed. “That right, Nate?”

“That’s why you’re hired,” Welch retorted. “You don’t like the money?”

“The money’s good.” Thorpe smiled.

Welch kicked again with his boot tip and said, “We’ll ride in nice an’ easy. When they come out we’ll have a little pow-wow.”

“They know you?” Thorpe asked him suddenly.

Welch looked at him. “Reckon they might know me,” he said. “Why?”

“Keep your head in,” Thorpe said, and he saw the color come to Welch’s face again.

“Supposin’ they don’t want to ride out?” Bannion asked.

“They’re ridin’ out,” Welch snapped.

Thorpe saw the slow smiles on the faces of the six hardcases as they stepped into the saddles again and rode off.

A half hour later they topped a rise and Thorpe

saw the dead town just ahead of them, lying at the base of a small bluff. A rusted railroad track led into it but stopped there, indicating that at one time this had been a railhead. There was nothing left now except a single straggly street of wooden structures, some of them already fallen in, but with many of the others intact.

The largest building in town was the hotel which stood a short distance up from the abandoned railroad station. They could see four horses tied to the tie rail in front of the hotel, a chestnut, a claybank, and two grays.

As they drew closer Thorpe saw the men sitting back in the shade under the hotel awning facing the main street. Welch said softly over his shoulder, "All right."

They rode into town past the railroad station and then on to the hotel. As they rode up to the tie rack, one of the men, a tall, gaunt fellow with a long jaw, stepped out to the edge of the porch. His long, slender hands were hooked in his gunbelt and he wore a Navy Colt gun low on the hip.

The tall man had a slit of a mouth and the coldest blue eyes Thorpe had ever seen. His hair was black, thick at the neck. He wore a black, flat-crowned hat, gray flannel shirt and faded blue Levi's. The heels of his boots were worn down.

"All right," he said, and then the recognition came to his eyes. "Nate," he said.

The three hardcases with Durango sat with their backs against the wall watching. This was the same breed as the men who rode with Welch. One man was small and stubby with a round face and a pudgy nose. The man next to him had slanted, Oriental eyes and a beak of a nose. The third man was big with reddish hair and tough blue eyes, and he wore a Mexican sombrero.

"What in hell you want, Nate?" Durango asked.

Thorpe distinctly heard Nate Welch clear his throat.

"Major Duveen is sendin' orders to you boys to move on," Welch growled.

At Thorpe's left Red Bannion was rolling a cigarette and watching the three men on the porch intently.

Durango's long face cracked into a cold smile. "The major worried?" he asked coolly.

"He's askin' you to move on," Nate told him.

"What if we don't?" Durango asked.

Thorpe said casually, "You will, mister."

Durango turned to look at him, his cold blue eyes flicking to the gun on Thorpe's hip.

"You'll know me the next time," Thorpe said.

"An' you'll know *me,* Bucko," Durango retorted.

Welch said, his tone petulant, "The major's askin' you to move on, Durango, an' quick."

"He rule the whole damn earth?" Durango asked flatly. "We move when we're ready, Welch."

The three men who had been sitting against the porch wall got up now, moving without haste. A thin smile came to Durango's lean face and he said softly, "If there's gonna be any shootin' in this town, Nate, you get it first. Kind of remember that."

The short fellow with the round face grinned, revealing broken teeth, and he said to Welch, "Through the gut, mister. You first."

They spread out on the porch facing the seven men on horseback. Only eight feet separated them from the D-Bar crew.

Nate Welch hesitated now, and because he hesitated he was lost, and he knew it. The fear was like little worms crawling around on his eyeballs. He sat there, the left shoulder sagging, making no move.

Because there were no orders, the six men with him sat motionless. Thorpe heard Bannion mumble something under his breath.

"You got your orders, Durango," Welch was saying, but there was no conviction in his voice.

"Go to hell," Durango told him pleasantly, "You an' the major."

The big fellow with the Mexican hat stepped out to the edge of the porch and looked at Thorpe who was directly in front of him. There was a grin on his face and not saying a word now, he drew his gun and fired a shot into the ground inches away from the front hoofs of the black.

Startled, the gelding lunged away, nearly unseating Thorpe. It took a few moments for Thorpe to regain his balance and control of the horse.

After he'd done so he dismounted, calmly tying the gelding to the tie rack, while the hardcase with the Mexican hat watched him.

Durango said, "Hadn't ought to have done that, Varney."

Varney grinned as he watched Thorpe duck under the rack and step toward the porch. He stood there, looking down at Thorpe and he said, "He ain't doin' nothin', Durango."

He holstered his gun and he was standing with his legs spread, looking down at Thorpe, whose head came to about his waist. Thorpe said easily, "Come on down, friend."

In reply Varney kicked out at his jaw with his right boot. It was a vicious, unexpected move, but Thorpe managed to pull his head back so that the tip of the boot merely grazed his chin.

Varney was offbalance after the kick, and Thorpe stepped in fast. He grasped him by the left ankle, and pulled hard, yanking him into the dirt. Varney let out a yell as he hit the ground, and he tried to pull his gun out of the holster.

Thorpe stepped forward to kick the gun out of

his grasp. Picking up the weapon and tossing it back into the road, Thorpe unbuckled his belt and said, “All right, Varney.”

Varney came up off the ground, cursing, and lunged in at him, head low. With his right fist Thorpe slashed Varney on the side of the head and then as he dropped, Thorpe brought up his knee full into the face.

Varney screamed and slumped forward into the dust, the blood pouring from both nostrils. Thorpe stepped back, waiting for him to get up, but Durango said casually,

“Reckon that’s it, mister.”

Thorpe nodded. Picking up the gunbelt he buckled it on again, conscious of the fact that Durango was watching him.

“Never saw anybody handle George Varney like that before,” he said.

Jug Hansen said, “You never saw anybody like this feller before, mister.”

Durango nodded. He said to Nate Welch, “You’re still not pushin’ us off, Nate, until we’re ready to go. Now you can make somethin’ out of that anyway you please.”

Welch glared at him. “You got your warning,” he said gruffly.

Durango smiled. “You did what you had to do, Nate, an’ it’s enough for you.”

Below him, George Varney was rolling on the ground, shaking his head, the blood still dripping.

He looked around now, his face bloodied and dirty, his eyes vacant.

Thorpe stepped up into the saddle and he said to Nate Welch, "Reckon this is as far as we're going, Welch. Let's pull out."

Welch turned his blue roan around. He said gruffly, vainly striving to save face, "You'll be seein' us, Durango, if you stay in this part of the country."

"Will I?" Durango smiled.

Varney was up on hands and knees now, shaking his head. He said dumbly, "Where is he? Where in hell is he?"

Welch rode off and the six men followed him down the street, leaving Durango and his two hardcases watching from the porch. Again, Thorpe rode at the rear with Red Bannion and as they were leaving town, Bannion said disgustedly, "He ain't near as tough as he figured he was, even with us behind him."

Thorpe smiled. He wondered what kind of report Welch would make when he returned to D-Bar. Nate had had a choice—back down or be dead, and he'd decided to back down.

Back at D-Bar Welch rode on to the ranch house while the hardcases returned to the bunkhouse. It was a half hour later when Thorpe spotted Welch coming toward the stable, his red face flustered. It was evident that the major had tongue-lashed him.

Welch saddled up and rode into town and after he was gone, Red Bannion said to Thorpe, "The major picked the wrong one to send after Durango."

Thorpe said nothing to this, but later on in the afternoon Major Duveen called to him from the verandah. Duveen's wide face was grim and the anger was still in his black eyes as he waited for Thorpe to come up.

He said tersely, "What happened in Avalon today?"

Thorpe smiled. "Durango told your ramrod to go to hell, major."

Duveen stared at him. "What about the rest of you?" he snapped.

"We take orders from Welch," Thorpe said. "Reckon he didn't have any to give."

Duveen took a cigar out of his pocket and put it in his mouth. He put a match to it and then he said offhandedly, "How did that Durango shape up to you?"

"He's tough," Thorpe said.

"Tough as you?" Duveen asked.

A smile came to Thorpe's lean face. "Reckon I wouldn't know," he said.

"You afraid of him? Plenty of people are?"

Thorpe shook his head. "I'm not afraid of him," he said.

Major Duveen looked past him toward the stable and then he touched a match to his cigar.

He said slowly, distinctly, "I want him dead. If you can do it there's five hundred dollars for you. No questions asked."

Thorpe frowned. "That's a hell of a lot of money," he stated.

"Don't worry about the money," Duveen said impatiently. "Can you do it?"

Thorpe rubbed his chin. "Why do you want him dead?" he asked.

Duveen stared, his eyes hard. "That's not part of the deal," he snapped. "There's five hundred dollars cash for you when I hear Durango's dead. Isn't that fair enough?"

Thorpe looked down at his boot tips.

"It's a job," Duveen was saying. "You've done jobs before."

Thorpe looked at him. "Reckon I'll think about it," he said.

Duveen said steadily, "When the man's dead you pick up your five hundred. That's all."

He went into the house. As Thorpe turned away he saw Lauren watching from one of the windows. He wondered if she'd heard what her husband had been saying, and, if she had, he wondered what she might think about it. She already had contempt for her husband. He wondered how long she would remain with him. Lauren was like a high-spirited horse. He didn't think Duveen would ever break her.

VI

Later on, Lauren strolled down to the stable and saw Thorpe inside, rubbing down the black. She came in, looked around and said, "Why was the major talking to you?"

Thorpe smiled. "Not about us," he said.

She frowned at him and she said tersely, "I don't want to see you friendly with him. He—he's a dog."

"You married him," Thorpe observed.

"I didn't know him," Lauren said. "Nobody really knows him. There's something on his mind which is eating at him all the time. It makes him wicked."

"What would be eating at him?" Thorpe asked her. "He has money, the biggest ranch in the territory, and a beautiful wife."

"That's not enough for him," Lauren said bitterly. "He wants to own everything, everybody. He thinks he's still in the military giving orders, but it's not going to work."

She turned, then, and strode out of the stable.

It was supper time when Leo Baines came into the bunkhouse and said, "Hear this Durango is in Benton now. Welch didn't scare him a damn bit."

"Durango won't scare," Thorpe smiled.

“That Varney would like to nail your hide to the wall,” Baines observed. “Reckon I wouldn’t ride into Benton alone any more. There’s four of ’em.”

Thorpe said, “I’m riding in tonight.”

Baines frowned and tugged at his lip. “You ask for it,” he complained. “You damn well ask for it all the time.”

After eating in the bunkhouse that evening, Thorpe smoked a cigarette through and went out to saddle the black. As he was doing so Baines, Bannion and Jug Hansen came in. Baines said, “Figured we’d ride into town.”

Thorpe smiled. “I can handle Varney,” he said.

“Not the four of ’em,” Baines said. “Nobody handles four, mister.”

They rode away from D-Bar at dusk and it was past eight when they raised the lights of Benton up ahead. This was a Friday night and the town was fairly crowded, much more so than the previous times Thorpe had been there.

He noticed the horses at the various tie racks as they moved down the main street. He spotted the four horses he’d seen tied at the rack in Avalon now tied in front of the Alhambra Saloon.

“In there,” Baines said, nodding.

Thorpe turned the black in toward the rack, the other three men following him. Leo Baines sat in the saddle as Thorpe dismounted and tied the black. He said, "You come in here just lookin' for a showdown with this crowd?"

"Maybe I just like the liquor in the Alhambra," he said, and he ducked under the tie rail.

It was more than the liquor, though. There was a dark-haired woman inside the building who looked at a man the way a man liked to be looked at, and he wanted to see more of her.

Sheriff Horner was standing on the porch as Thorpe went up, and the tall lawman with the pepper-colored hair nodded and said, "Reckon you like this town, mister."

"A good town," Thorpe nodded and walked inside.

Durango and the three hardcases with him had apparently been in Benton for some time, and, having had their drinks at the bar, were now playing cards at a corner table. Durango spotted Thorpe immediately as he came in through the bat-wing doors and his tough blue eyes flicked.

Hallie Grant greeted Thorpe at the bar. No one was within hearing range of them and she said in a low voice, "Hear anything?"

Thorpe shook his head. "Duveen wants a man by the name of Durango dead. That mean anything to you?"

Hallie looked at him. "Durango's here," she said without looking toward their table.

"Anything else?" Thorpe asked. "He new in this town?"

"He's been here off and on," Hallie explained. "He's like the others—a drifter. I haven't seen him, though, for almost a year."

"Why would Duveen want him killed?" Thorpe asked.

Again Hallie shook her head. "He could kill you," she said. "Durango's gun is supposed to be the fastest in this part of the country."

Thorpe inclined his head slightly, but made no comment.

Baines, Bannion and Hansen came in, pulling up at the bar nearby. Thorpe said to them, "Drinks on me seeing as how you're protecting me."

The bartender brought a bottle and glasses, and Hallie said to Thorpe, "What are you going to do about Durango?"

"Talk first," Thorpe told her. "Any place I can meet him here in private?"

He noticed that Durango was watching him from the table. George Varney was watching, too, his nose plastered with tape, the hatred showing in his eyes.

"There's a back room with a card game going on in it," Hallie said. "When they clear out you have it." She added thoughtfully, "What happened to Durango's friend? He rode in here looking for a doctor for his broken nose."

"Maybe he bumped into a wall," Thorpe said soberly. "Reckon you can get Durango in that room tonight?"

"I'll give him the message," Hallie told him. "What about the other three."

Thorpe glanced at the three D-Bar riders at the bar nearby and he said, "They won't get in."

He moved off, then, stepping into the private gambling room at the other end of the saloon. Picking up an old newspaper, he sat down in a corner and started to read.

When he'd finished the paper he pulled up closer to the game and watched. When one of the players pulled out and he was invited in, he shook his head.

An hour later the game broke up and as the players filed out of the room, Thorpe picked up the cards and started to shuffle them. He was laying the cards out on the table in solitaire fashion fifteen minutes later when Durango stepped into the room, closing the door behind him.

He stood against the door for a moment, looking down at Thorpe, his cold blue eyes narrowed.

"You wanted to see me," he said.

Thorpe laid down the deck. "Sit down," he said.

Durango sat down across from him and he said, "You busted up my man good. Now you want to see me. You're Duveen's rider, ain't you?"

Thorpe nodded. "Duveen wants to pay me five hundred dollars to see you dead," he said. "Figured you'd like to know."

Durango looked at him steadily for a moment and then he laughed mirthlessly. “You’re telling me about it,” he said.

Thorpe nodded.

“Why?” Durango asked curiously. “You made a deal.”

Thorpe shrugged. “I might take five hundred from you,” he said, “to kill *him.*”

Durango’s mouth opened and then closed again. He said, “You figure he’d be easier to kill than me?”

Thorpe picked up the cards and shuffled them. He said, “I’m just damn curious to know why Duveen wants you dead.”

He looked up suddenly and he saw Durango staring at him, his face tight.

“You ask a hell of a lot of questions,” he said tersely.

Thorpe shrugged again. “A man’s curious when he sees somebody put five hundred on the line like that.”

“Maybe I stole some stock,” Durango said. “Maybe I took him in a crooked card game.”

And maybe you rode with him when he raided a paymaster’s wagon, disguised as an Indian, Thorpe was thinking bitterly, *and made off with a quarter million dollars, and you left Tom Halloran scalped on the ground.*

Durango was saying, “When I want Duveen dead, I’ll do it myself, friend.”

Thorpe lay the cards on the table and said nothing.

"You figure on collecting Duveen's five hundred on me?" Durango asked him softly.

"A man might be a damned fool trying to do that." Thorpe smiled.

"A *dead* damned fool," Durango retorted. He stood up and he said, "George Varney ain't forgetting either what you did to him, Jack. He don't forget easy."

"That's all right," Thorpe said, and he was laying out the cards again, when Durango went out.

Thorpe left the room a few minutes later and went back to the bar. Then he dropped in at a card game where the three D-Bar riders were playing.

Bannion said, "You're keepin' queer company, Coleman. You figure on playin' this horse win an' lose?"

"Always play to win." Thorpe told him. He noticed now that Durango and his riders had left.

Horner was at the bar with Hallie Grant having a chat before starting his rounds of the town. When he'd gone Thorpe went up to the bar and Hallie said to him, "You found nothing; you learned nothing."

Thorpe shook his head. "I'm figuring Durango was in on that raid which is why Duveen wants him out of the way. Durango is figuring there are plenty of those greenbacks still around and he's curious. Maybe none of them except Duveen really knew how much was in the paymaster's trunks when that raid was made. Now they're wondering, and now they're coming back."

"And the major is hiring hardcase riders for protection," Hallie nodded.

"That's the way it's beginning to shape up," Thorpe nodded. "Duveen made his deal with the crowd he had, and paid them off when it was over. None of them figured he was taking that kind of money."

"The money isn't doing him any good," Hallie observed.

Thinking of Lauren, Thorpe nodded.

"If I were you," Hallie said, changing the subject, "I'd watch that man with the broken nose. He's had his eyes on you all evening. You do that to his nose?"

"He tried to play," Thorpe said gravely. "I'm obliged for the help from you."

He stepped to the door and then stood there, looking out into the street. Directly across the road four men stood in front of an empty store. Their cigarettes glowed in the shadows. On the face of one of them was a white patch. They were waiting for him to come out. The four horses on which they'd ridden into town were still tied at the rack to Thorpe's right.

Easily, Thorpe pushed out through the doors and came out to the edge of the porch. He was standing there when he heard the doors swing behind him and there were footsteps on the wood.

Red Bannion said, “Waitin’ for you, ain’t they?”

“They’re waiting,” Thorpe nodded.

Bannion, Baines and Hansen ranged up alongside him. Across the road the four men on the opposite walk were facing them. A rider came down the street moving between them.

Thorpe said, “You boys wait here. If Varney wants it he’ll come off by himself.”

Bannion said, “He’ll come.”

Thorpe shrugged. He moved away from the porch, walking leisurely and looking across the road as he went down the boardwalk. Now he saw the man with the white bandage on his face step away from the other three and move in the same direction. Durango and the two men with him stayed where they were.

Thorpe kept walking, watching the man across the way. He stepped around a drunk on the walk and passed two lighted saloon fronts. Across the way George Varney passed a patch of light out in front of the Roseland Dancehall.

When they reached the corner Thorpe stopped. Instead of crossing at the intersection he stepped out into the road and he stood there, waiting, facing Varney on the opposite corner.

A buckboard came by, the driver staring at Thorpe curiously, and then seeing Varney across the road, he whipped up his team and rattled on.

Varney waited across the road, staring over at Thorpe. Thorpe couldn't see his face as he was now in the shadows. He was still up on the walk, though, hesitating as Nate Welch had hesitated in Avalon, and watching him Thorpe knew that he wasn't stepping down.

Thorpe gave him plenty of time but it wasn't time George Varney needed. It was something inside—deep down, something he was lacking at the moment, maybe something which had gone out of him with the blood spilling from his nose.

Suddenly, Varney swung around and headed back toward where Durango and the other two men were waiting and watching. Thorpe stepped back on to the walk and then he headed back toward the Alhambra.

When he came up, Bannion said dryly, "Wasn't much of a damn fight."

"It wasn't a fight he wanted," Thorpe observed.

He watched Varney angling across the road to where they'd left their horses. He walked alone, Durango and the other two watching him, and Thorpe had his moment of pity for the man: Varney was finished.

The tall fellow with the Mexican sombrero mounted, yanked the horse's head around savagely, and rode off, not even looking at Thorpe as he went by the Alhambra.

Leo Baines said, "He ain't through with you. Look for it in the back now."

Thorpe nodded. He watched Durango and the other two men crossing toward them. When Durango came up on the walk, pausing in front of Thorpe before going on into the saloon, he said, "You scared that one, my friend."

Thorpe nodded.

"You busted him up," Durango went on, "and you took the heart out of him. That's all it was."

Red Bannion said, "Reckon that was enough, mister."

"It won't work on me," Durango said and he entered the saloon.

Thorpe watched him go and then he moved toward the tie rack. "Headin' back," he said.

The four of them rode out of town and as they were passing the last house on the street Jug Hansen said, "That Varney wasn't as big as he figured he was."

"He's alive," Bannion observed, "an' that's what he figured on bein' tonight."

"That's somethin'," Leo Baines chortled. "It's better than nothin'."

VII

They were two miles out of Benton, heading back to D-Bar, following the stage road which passed along the base of a bluff. They were in the shadows of the bluff until they came out again, and the sliver of moon picked them up.

Thorpe was slightly in the lead with Baines almost abreast of him on his right side. It was Baines who cried out sharply when the rifle cracked, and a bullet grazed the back of his neck, breaking the skin.

Whipping his gun out of the holster, Thorpe slid to the ground, moving the weapon in the direction from which the shot had come.

"On top the bluff," Red Bannion called.

They were all off the saddles now, guns out, waiting.

Leo Baines held a bandanna to his bleeding neck, cursed, and said one word, "Varney."

Thorpe could hear a horse running off in the night, moving hard on the far side of the bluff. He said to Baines, "You all right?"

"Reckon that was for you, mister," Baines told him. "You're a damned dangerous man to travel with."

Thorpe holstered his gun and stepped into the saddle. Before riding in pursuit he said quietly,

"Only one of them now. Reckon you boys better ride on."

"Good hunting," Bannion said to him as he moved away up the bluff.

Thorpe knew as he rode off that he wasn't coming back or stopping until he'd settled this with George Varney. There was no other way. Varney's pride had been dragged in the dust tonight and destroyed, and the wound could only be assuaged in the blood of the man who'd destroyed him.

Having missed his shot tonight, Varney would try again and again until he succeeded or was dead himself. Thorpe had seen it happen to other men.

Crossing the bluff, Thorpe could hear Varney's horse still moving very fast. Varney was traveling south over the open range and Thorpe rode after him.

Knowing that it might be a long ride, he didn't push the black too hard. He rode at a steady pace, listening for Varney's horse up ahead. Once he caught a glimpse of the man in the starlight as he topped a low hill up ahead. Varney was still heading south and toward the west now. The dead town of Avalon lay toward the southwest and there was a good possibility that Varney was heading in that direction.

Thorpe figured the time to be somewhat past midnight. There was a sliver of moon riding high in the sky and plenty of starlight to go by. Even without the starlight or the moon he could have followed Varney by the dust kicked up by his horse.

There was no shooting as they were still too far apart. The longer they rode the more convinced Thorpe became that Varney was heading toward Avalon where he would make some kind of stand. Varney would have known by now that only one man was on his trail.

For an hour they rode on with Varney still some distance ahead, and Thorpe came upon Avalon quite unexpectedly. Topping a rise Thorpe, suddenly saw it below and had a glimpse of Varney pounding into the main street, past the railroad station, and up to the hotel where they'd been sitting.

It was time for caution now as there were a thousand places in which Varney could hide, a thousand ambushes he could set up. Thorpe pulled up, letting the black breathe. On the brow of the hill he dismounted, squatted down on his heels, and rolled a cigarette. He smoked it through before riding on again.

He was convinced that Varney wasn't going any farther than this. He'd come straight here after firing the shot from the bluff. Now he would try it again.

Riding the black down to the railroad station, Thorpe dismounted and led the horse in under a wagon shed nearby. Then he moved up to the street and stood in the shadows against the wall of the building, looking down toward the hotel.

The dust kicked up by Varney's horse still hung in the air. He was not sure of the building into which Varney had gone even though he'd dismounted near the hotel. Varney was watching now from a window or doorway, ready to pump bullets into his man when he came down the street.

Pulling back, Thorpe loosened the gun in the holster. Then he swung around behind the railroad station, crossed a small switching yard, and stepped into a backyard behind one of the buildings on the main street.

Stepping in through the rear door of the nearest building, he moved down a narrow corridor, and, in the dim shadows there, stumbled into a staircase which led to the second floor. He went up the stairs slowly, gun in hand, realizing that there was a possibility that Varney had crossed the road and was in this building. It was more likely, though, that Varney was in a building farther down.

Moving into one of the rooms, Thorpe felt the cool night air coming in through one of the windows which opened on to a rear shed. Stepping to the window, Thorpe looked out. He noticed that the ledge of the roof was only a foot above the top of the window frame.

Carefully now, to avoid making the slightest bit of noise, he stepped out on to the window sill and then reached up and grasped the edge of the roof. Bracing one boot against the broken window frame, he hoisted himself up on the roof. Thorpe crouched there for a moment before moving up toward the front of the building.

There was a foot-high parapet overlooking the street, and Thorpe crawled up toward the ledge. Lifting his head carefully now, he looked down into the street.

Nothing moved. Starlight and moonlight reflected on some of the unbroken windows across the way. A signboard above a saloon squeaked as a light breeze touched it. There were no other sounds in this ghost town.

He lay for some time on the edge of the roof, peering down into the street. An hour passed as he sat on the roof. The quarter moon had swung around until it was now directly behind him. When he raised his head now to look down into the street again, he became aware of an unusual movement out in the middle of the road.

It took a moment for him to realize that the movement was the shadow of his head over the parapet as he looked down. The thought occurred to him that if he could see his own shadow down in the street, very possibly some one else watching from a window or another roof also could see it.

He dropped his head behind the parapet just as a rifle cracked from an upper floor window in a building diagonally across from the one on which he was hidden. He saw the orange-red flash of the gun as the slug gouged wood off the rim of the parapet inches from where his face had been a moment ago.

Throwing his body away from the edge of the roof, Thorpe lay flat on his back, looking up at the stars. He'd made a slight mistake and he'd nearly been killed because of it. He would have to be more careful tonight if he wanted to stay alive.

He lay still for some time just looking up at the stars and then he began to work his way back toward the rear of the roof. Reaching it, he lowered himself, dropped lightly to the shed roof below, and then descended from there to the ground.

Varney had fired that single shot from the window above the saloon with a squeaking signboard, but probably he had shifted his position by now and was setting himself up in another part of town. It meant that he had to be rooted out again.

Moving behind the buildings on his side of the street, Thorpe progressed the entire length of the town until he came to a dilapidated shed. He moved out to the edge of the building, crouched, and then suddenly ran across the road, dropping behind a mass of rubble which once had been a building. He was now on the same side of the street as Varney, but he still could not be sure in which house Varney was hiding, nor was he sure Varney had not seen him dart across the road.

Sliding around the rubble pile, Thorpe stepped into a narrow alley and waited there before going on again. He watched every footstep now, making sure that he made no noise as he walked along at the rear of the buildings.

As he paused once at the far end of an alley and looked up toward the street, he saw a man with a rifle suddenly run across the mouth of the alley, heading in the opposite direction from the one he, himself, was taking.

Carefully, he stepped back toward the rear entrance of the building he'd just passed. The door itself was gone and a damp odor assailed his nostrils as he stood in the entrance way.

Very distinctly he heard a door open at the far end of the building and then light footsteps on the wooden floor. Flattening himself against the wall, gun in hand, Thorpe waited.

They were in the same building at last and he had the advantage.

They'd entered a two-story building, and now he heard Varney going up the stairs lightly, rapidly, the treads squeaking beneath his weight. This posed another problem and Thorpe frowned as he waited in the rear of the house. With Varney on the second floor it was going to be impossible to ascend those stairs without alerting him.

Up above he could hear Varney shifting his weight around, moving from one window to another to look out. One step at a time, Thorpe came out of the entrance way, pausing just outside. Above him were several second-floor windows, and, as he flattened himself against the wall, he heard Varney come to the rear window to look out.

He waited until he heard Varney move again toward the front of the street to look for signs of him there. About thirty feet from the house was a broken-down picket fence casting a long shadow on the ground. Thorpe darted out toward the fence and sat with his back against it, facing the rear windows of the house. He sat with his Colt gun across his knees, waiting, knowing that Varney would be coming back to the rear periodically to look out. When he did, he was never going to get back to the front again.

Varney took his time about checking the rear of the house, though. Fully ten minutes elapsed before Thorpe saw his shadowy form at the open window.

Varney leaned back against the window frame cautiously for a few moments, and then with his big hat removed, he leaned out slightly to look up and down along the rear of the buildings.

Steadying the gun on his knee, Thorpe said, "All right, George."

Varney had been holding the rifle with both hands as he leaned out the window. Desperately, he swung it toward Thorpe now, squeezing on the trigger at the same time. The rifle roared and the slug ripped through the board fence to Thorpe's right.

Knowing that he could not miss at this distance, Thorpe sent his first shot. Varney suddenly lunged forward, his head and shoulders out of the window, the rifle dropping from his grasp. He hung there in the window for several moments, hat falling from his head, arms dangling, and then very slowly he slid out the window, landing with a thud in front of the rear entrance.

Thorpe got up and walked forward. Bending down, he rolled Varney over, had his look at the man in the starlight, and then stood up. With the dirty bandages across Varney's broken nose, his face had been a literal death mask.

It was almost dawn when Thorpe rode up to D-Bar. Red Bannion was sitting on the bench in front of the bunkhouse smoking a cigar. He watched Thorpe ride by to the stable, dismount, and walk the black inside.

As Thorpe came up to the bunkhouse Bannion said, "Find him?"

"Found him," Thorpe nodded.

Bannion thought about that for a moment and then he said, "That Varney was no damn good anyway. You turnin' in?"

Again Thorpe nodded. He was tired now and it had been a long day.

Bannion said speculatively, “Hell to pay around here. Major’s lady pulled out an’ left him tonight. Drove in to Benton.”

Thorpe stared at the gunman. “Pulled out?” he repeated.

“That’s what I hear,” Bannion told him. “Had another argument an’ she got into the buckboard an’ drove into town. She’s stayin’ at the hotel now.”

Thorpe considered this matter. He’d anticipated that Lauren would leave the major sooner or later, but he hadn’t thought it would be this soon.

Bannion said, “Get your sleep.”

Thorpe went into the bunkhouse, kicked off his boots, and lay down on the bunk. When he awoke it was near noon and Jug Hansen was saying, “Coffee’s on an’ the major’s askin’ for you.”

Thorpe had his coffee and then crossed to the house, finding Major Duveen and Nate Welch sitting on the porch. Welch stared, the unfriendliness in his green eyes. He said, “Hear you did in one o’ Durango’s boys last night.”

Thorpe nodded. “He tried to bushwhack me.”

Duveen said quietly, “What about Durango?”

“Reckon he’s still alive,” Thorpe told him.

Welch said, “You figure Durango will come after you for what you did to his man?”

Thorpe shrugged. "I don't figure it that way," he said.

Duveen frowned. "Think about that five hundred," he said by way of dismissal.

Thorpe said softly, "That offer out to Welch, too?"

He saw the red come to Welch's face. The D-Bar ramrod said stiffly, "You got a way of handling your tongue, mister."

Thorpe just nodded to him and turned and went down the steps, crossing toward the stable.

That afternoon when Duveen rode in to Benton, Nate Welch signed off three of the hardcases to go along with him. Leo Baines, Dave Shaw and Jug Hansen pulled out of the card game reluctantly and saddled up.

Thorpe watched Red Bannion play solitaire in the bunkhouse for some time. Then at dusk he walked toward the table, noticing as he did so that the ranch house was in darkness. Always, there had been lights on because Lauren had liked the light.

Bannion came in as Thorpe was saddling the gelding, and he said, "Reckon I'm ridin' with you, you don't mind."

Thorpe shrugged. "Free town," he said. "Come ahead."

Bannion said, "You figure Duveen went in after his wife?"

“She won’t come back,” Thorpe said with conviction, and he wondered what Duveen would do about that, a man accustomed to giving orders and seeing them obeyed. Probably for the first time in his adult life Major Bennett Duveen was trying to cope with a problem which was beyond him, and Thorpe was curious to see how far he would go.

VIII

They reached Benton some time after dark and Thorpe spotted Duveen's buckboard tied up out in front of the hotel. When they rode on down to the Alhambra they spotted Leo Baines standing out on the porch watching them dismount.

Bannion said, "What's new?"

Baines grinned. "Duveen," he said. "Loadin' up. Never saw him doin' it afore. Not like this, anyway."

Thorpe stepped toward the bat-wing doors and looked inside. He saw Duveen at a table with Nate Welch. Jug Hansen lounged at the bar nearby, a frown on his wide face.

There was a nearly-empty bottle and two glasses on the table between Duveen and Welch. Welch also was frowning, obviously displeased with his employer.

There was little doubt that Major Duveen had been drinking heavily this night. His face was a deep, almost purple color. His head rested on his wide shoulders, his heavy chin was lowered, and the drink was in his eyes.

Even as Thorpe watched, the major slapped the table with his hand, ordering a bartender to bring him another bottle.

Red Bannion said to Leo Baines, "She turn him down?"

Baines shrugged. "He was in the hotel a while," he said, "an' then he come out. He come alone so I don't figure she jumped when he cracked the whip—not this time."

"Durango in town?" Thorpe asked.

"Ain't seen him," Baines told him, "an' that's who I'm supposed to be watchin' for out here. Welch's orders."

Thorpe looked up and down the street, his eyes stopping on the buckboard out in front of the hotel, and then he said to Bannion, "Have a drink on me, Red." He walked off in the direction of the hotel with Bannion and Baines staring after him.

Stepping into the hotel lobby, Thorpe moved up to the desk and said, "Mrs. Duveen's room."

The clerk frowned at him, shrugged, and said, "No. 21, second floor."

Thorpe went up the stairs and down along the corridor until he came to room No. 21. He knocked on the door, noticing as he did so that there was a crack of light underneath.

"Who is it?" Lauren asked, her voice shrill.

"Coleman," Thorpe said.

Lauren opened the door and looked out. She was swaying slightly, the light from the lamp beyond illuminating her blond hair. He could smell the liquor on her as she stood in front of him.

"You," Lauren said, seemingly quite pleased. "Come in."

Thorpe walked in, closing the door behind him. He held his hat in his hand and he looked down at her as she stood a short distance away. "You're drunk," he said.

"Wouldn't you be?" she countered.

"He want you to come back?" Thorpe asked her.

"I'll never go back," Lauren said grimly. "Never—never."

She paused and then she said wickedly, "Besides, I know something about him now and I'll never go back."

Thorpe's gray eyes flicked. "You know something you didn't know before?" he asked.

"I know," Lauren told him, and she came forward and put both hands on his shoulders, looking up into his face.

"What do you know?" Thorpe asked as if in jesting. "You know where he got his money?"

Lauren grimaced. "You know, too?" she asked.

Thorpe shook his head. "I'm asking," he said. "*You* know."

Lauren turned away toward the table. "He'd kill me if I told any one," she said in a low voice. "He'd kill me. I saw it in his eyes."

"He want you to come back?" Thorpe asked her.

"He said he wouldn't let me leave this town," Lauren half-whispered. "He won't even let me leave the room. He's afraid I—I'll say something."

Thorpe looked at the bottle on the table and the glass. He said, "You're trying to run away by hitting that bottle. You can't keep that up forever, you know."

Lauren swung around on him, her green eyes wild. "Get me out of here," she whispered. "Please help me out of here!"

She went over to him again and she put her arms around his neck. "Please," she said again.

"We'll see," Thorpe told her. "Reckon I wouldn't try to leave if I were you."

Lauren was weeping drunkenly when he left. This time as he crossed the lobby he noticed Dave Shaw sitting in a far corner, a newspaper drawn up across his face. Shaw had been there when Thorpe had come into the hotel and he was there for a purpose.

Walking over to him, Thorpe took a cigar from his pocket and held it out. Shaw, a tall, gaunt man with a thin face, said, "Obliged."

"Duveen put you here to watch his woman?" Thorpe asked him.

Shaw nodded glumly. "Hell of a business," he said. "Hell of a job, but the pay is good."

"She's full of liquor," Thorpe said. "I don't figure she'll do any running."

"When a woman don't want me," Shaw observed, "I say, to hell with her, an' let her run."

"You're not Duveen," Thorpe smiled, and he turned and went out into the street.

On the walk he saw Durango leaning against the post facing the hotel entrance. His hat was pushed back on his head and his lean hands were hooked in his gunbelt.

As Thorpe slowed down in front of him, Durango said idly, "See you got Varney."

Thorpe nodded. "He had the first shot," he said.

Durango smiled. "Most of 'em do," he observed, "an' Varney was a damned fool, anyway. He made his own coffin when he tried to push you."

Thorpe said nothing to this. He was about to go on when Durango pulled him up with a question.

"You still after Duveen's five hundred?"

Thorpe looked down at the walk. "You'd like to know," he said.

"Every man likes to know if he's gettin' a bullet in the back," Durango said.

"It won't be in the back," Thorpe said and he walked off.

As he moved down the street he saw Major Duveen coming toward him. Nate Welch was on one side of him, with Leo Baines following in the rear. Duveen walked stiffly, stolidly, and he walked without the slightest weaving motion despite the drink in him.

As Thorpe stepped aside to let them pass, Duveen looked at him steadily, his solid jaw set tight, and he said, "Get the hell out of my way."

He went on and Thorpe smiled after him. Leo Baines coming on behind him just shook his head at Thorpe.

In the Alhambra Saloon Hallie Grant said to Thorpe at the bar, "There's something eating him. He's done this a few times before. Came in and drank enough for three men and then walked out as steady as a judge."

"He's trying to forget," Thorpe said grimly.

"Now he has his troubles with his wife," Hallie observed, "and if I'm not mistaken she's already asked you for help."

Thorpe smiled faintly. "She wants help," he nodded.

"If you give it to her," Hallie warned him, "you're dead. I suppose you know that, too."

Thorpe shrugged.

Red Bannion came in then and said, "Duveen's pullin' out. You figure on ridin' along now?"

"Later," Thorpe told him.

Bannion looked at him and smiled. "Reckon we'll wait, too," he said. "No damn rush gettin' back."

They played a few hands of cards and as they were playing Thorpe heard the nightstage roll up to the Wells-Fargo station down the street. He thought nothing of it until Dave Shaw walked into the Alhambra a half hour later, a frown on his face. Shaw went up to the bar, had himself a drink, and then came and sat down at their table, taking the bottle and glass with him.

"Walkin' off your job, Dave?" Bannion asked him.

"Hell with the job," Shaw scowled. "Hell with Duveen, too." He poured himself another drink.

"She still there?" Thorpe asked as he looked at his cards.

"Took off," Shaw told him, "an' to hell with Duveen again."

Thorpe put his cards down on the table. "She left the hotel?" he asked.

"Came down with her bag an' took that east-bound stage," Dave Shaw told him. He added tersely, "No damn job for a man, keepin' watch on a woman. Duveen wants her, he should o' kept her at the ranch."

Thorpe said quickly, "Anybody else know Mrs. Duveen took that stage out?"

"Damned if I know," Shaw said glumly. "Nate Welch was still in town. He didn't go out with Duveen. Saw him near the hotel."

Thorpe pushed his chair back. He said to Bannion, "Cash in my chips, Red."

"Where you goin'?" Bannion asked, surprised.

"Stay here," Thorpe said.

He rode the black out of town at a fast pace. It was nearly half an hour since the stage had left Benton and it could have covered quite a distance with six good horses in the traces.

Face grim, Thorpe moved over a rise, pounding

down the stage road, moving due east. He passed one rider moving at a leisurely pace ahead of him, a rider who turned and stared in surprise.

The same quarter-moon hung up in the sky that he'd seen in Avalon the previous night, and the sky was studded with stars. The black was moving at an easy, ground-consuming pace and the road here was good.

An hour or so after leaving Benton he saw the lights of the coach far up ahead of him. He noticed immediately that the lights were not moving, the stage apparently having come to a stop.

The black hammered on down the road and Thorpe let the animal run. He noticed now that the lights were moving again, but not away from him. The driver had swung the stage off the road, made his turn, and was now heading back toward Benton.

Thorpe sensed then what had happened and it made him sick. The stage driver pulled up as Thorpe approached. He had his shotgun raised and waiting and he yelled, "Hold it up, Jack. Don't come too damn close."

Thorpe pulled up the black.

"You have a woman passenger aboard?" he asked quickly.

The driver stared down at him, his face dimly revealed in the light from the coach lamps on either side of the seat.

"Reckon that's why I'm turnin' back to Benton," he said grimly. "Bunch jumped this rig a pace up the road an' took the lady out. Sounded to me like she'd been drinkin' pretty heavy."

"Where are they?" Thorpe asked him quickly.

"Damn if I know," the driver scowled. "They took her an' rode off. Had me covered all the time—three of 'em. I couldn't get this greener up. I'm headin' back to Benton to tell the sheriff."

"Which way did they go?" Thorpe asked him.

The driver motioned toward the north. "One of 'em was ridin' double with the lady," he said. "They won't be goin' too fast, mister. Couldn't see who they were. They had bandannas over their faces."

Thorpe pulled away from the stage and rode on up the road, looking for tracks now—the tracks of three horses heading north away from the stage road.

Fifty yards east of the spot where he'd met the coach he picked up the tracks.

It wasn't too difficult following the trail made by the three riders who'd abducted Lauren Duveen, and Thorpe had no doubt that he'd be able to catch up with them fairly soon, burdened as they were with one horse carrying double. Besides, they wouldn't be expecting pursuit so quickly and they wouldn't be in any particular rush.

The trail led due north up into the hills, skirting

a series of ridges to the east. Once or twice Thorpe had to dismount and strike a match to make sure he was on the trail.

They moved through a patch of timber on one occasion and Thorpe had to circle slightly to find the trail on the other side. Then they went over a gravel stream, and as the black came out of the water, hoofs digging into the sandy soil, Thorpe saw the huddled shape on the ground nearby.

The riders had probably paused here to water the horses and then they'd gone on again but they'd left something behind. Thorpe walked a few yards down along the stream. Lauren Duveen lay on her face, her left arm outstretched and right hand under her. She was wearing the dress Thorpe had seen her wearing in the hotel room, a tan dress with a white collar.

She'd been shot through the head. When he held the match closer he could see the round, blue bullet hole through the forehead with almost no blood coming from the wound.

Shaking out the match, he stood up and walked back to where he'd left the gelding. He had only this consolation that Lauren had never known what was coming. When she'd been taken from the stage she'd still been in a stupor. Whatever she'd known about Major Bennett Duveen was now gone forever.

Stepping into the saddle Thorpe rode on again following the trail of the three riders. They seemed to be moving along at a much faster rate now, still going north but now seeming to veer somewhat toward the west.

On two occasions during the night he lost the trail and had to backtrack and circle before he was able to pick it up again. He never knew when the third man parted from the other two. But near dawn when he spotted the tiny cookfire up ahead he saw only two men crouching in front of it, boiling their coffee.

They'd built this fire at the edge of a tiny grove of cottonwoods because they'd evidently found water here, the first water they'd found since leaving the stream where Lauren had been killed.

Moving forward on foot now, Thorpe loosened the gun in his belt, circling around behind the grove. He saw the two horses tied at the edge of the grove. The horse standing in the patch of light from the fire was a steel-gray. He could not make out the color of the second animal.

Stepping in among the trees he began to move in closer, passing from one large tree to another until he was within fifteen yards of the fire. He paused here to have a look at the two killers and he did not recognize either one of them.

The man facing him was a little rat-faced chap with an evil, twisted mouth; the second man was taller, heavier, his jaw covered with a stubble of black beard. Both men wore guns on their hips, and the smaller man wore a tattered black hat with a broken rim.

Thorpe recognized the type, typical cut-throats who'd been paid good money tonight to do a dirty job. The man who'd paid them had taken off in another direction, leaving the two killers still pushing to get out of the country.

The big fellow with the stubble beard was sipping coffee out of a tin cup and the smaller man was poking at the fire with a stick when Thorpe stepped out from behind the trees and walked forward silently, quickly, making no effort to conceal himself now.

The bearded man spotted him first and he threw the cup away, letting out a yell as he straightened up, and grabbing at the gun on his hip. The shorter man backed away from the fire so hastily that he fell, yelled, and then scrambled to his feet.

The taller man got off the first shot, a hurried one which went wide of the mark. Thorpe's bullet struck him just above the belt buckle and he doubled up, staggered, and then sat down. The gun fell from his hand as he clutched his stomach.

The smaller man was almost shrieking in fear as he sent lead in Thorpe's direction. He tried to back up at the same time, stumbling and falling again as he shot.

One bullet grazed Thorpe's left arm; another went over his head. Then Thorpe shot him through the head with the first bullet and put a second through his chest as he was going down. He was dead immediately.

The fellow with the beard still sat on the ground, clutching his stomach, his eyes glazing, staring at Thorpe who now came into the fire-light, gun in hand.

With his boot Thorpe kicked away the man's gun and then he said, "Who paid you to kill a woman?"

The bearded man stared up at him, and there was hatred in his yellow eyes. He said in almost a whisper, "Go to hell, Jack," and then he died, pitching forward slowly on his face, his hat falling from his head and into the fire where it began to smolder.

Thorpe stepped up and kicked the hat away, not even thinking about the act. He stood there for several moments looking down at the two dead men. The coffee pot was bubbling over the coals at one corner of the fire, the rich, strong aroma assailing his nostrils.

Filling the tin cup nearby, he drank it with his back toward the fire looking toward the east where the first rays of light were coming into the sky. When he finished the cup he tossed it away, unsaddled the two horses and let them run, and then he stepped into the saddle again and rode south in the direction of Benton.

He was an hour from the camp where he'd

intercepted the two killers when Sheriff Ben Horner and four posse men rode toward him. Horner stared at him, the question in his gray eyes.

"Find them?" he asked.

Thorpe nodded and jerked his head over his shoulder. "Hour's ride back along my trail," he said. "You see Mrs. Duveen?"

Horner nodded. "Hell of a business," he scowled. "Who were they?"

"Drifters," Thorpe told him. "Dogs. They were paid to do a job."

"By who?"

"They're not sayin' any more," Thorpe said, and he rode past the five men.

IX

It was high noon when he rode the jaded black into Benton. Instead of riding on to D-Bar he walked the black into the stable behind the hotel, had the boy look after the animal, and then came out on the street for a late breakfast in a nearby restaurant.

Before leaving Benton, considerably later in the afternoon, he'd seen the buckboard rolling in with Lauren Duveen's body under a tarpaulin. Ben Horner had ridden out of town earlier, and Thorpe assumed the sheriff was heading for D-Bar to inform the major.

Also, before leaving Benton, Thorpe paused at the Alhambra for a word with Hallie.

"They killed her," Hallie said when he sat with her at a table. "Who?"

"I figure Welch," Thorpe scowled. "It's the kind of work he would do."

Hallie stared at him. "You don't think the major ordered it?" she asked.

Thorpe shook his head. "Can't figure Welch doing it on his own, either," he said, "unless he had some damn good reasons. The way I look at it, Duveen didn't want his wife to leave him. He wanted her back."

"What will he do now?" Hallie wanted to know.

"There'll be hell to pay some where down the line," Thorpe stated. "I'm headin' back to D-Bar. Durango still in town?"

Hallie shook her head. "I haven't seen him," she said. "They may have ridden out." She paused and she said, "You're sure it was the major now in this payroll business?"

Thorpe looked at her. "What do you think?" he countered. "Lauren knew something. Now she's dead for it."

"I wouldn't want to hang a man on what I know," Hallie said quietly, "but I wouldn't want to see him ride off, either."

"He's not ridin' off," Thorpe said, "not from this one."

"Stay alive yourself," Hallie murmured. "That's important, too."

"To you?" Thorpe asked her, looking her full in the face.

"To me," she nodded simply.

Ben Horner's buckskin horse was tied up in front of the ranch house when Thorpe rode up to the stable, but he didn't see Horner. Red Bannion came out of the bunkhouse, crossed to the stable, and looked at Thorpe curiously.

"Hear you had a little excitement last night," he said. "Hell of a business, shootin' down a woman."

"How is the major taking it?" Thorpe asked curiously.

"Drunk," Bannion told him. "Stone, blind drunk, an' has been since last night. Welch an' Horner are in with him."

"Welch," Thorpe said and Bannion glanced at him.

"Nate wouldn't have the nerve to kill Mrs. Duveen," Bannion observed.

"Unless he had a damned good reason," Thorpe growled.

They were standing in front of the stable when the door of the ranch house burst open and Major Duveen strode out, his face red and sweaty, his heavy jaw thrust out, his dark hair mussed.

Welch was trying to talk to the major as Duveen strode across the yard but Duveen wasn't listening. Horner came on behind them, frowning.

Despite the quantity of liquor he'd consumed, Duveen was still steady on his feet, a remarkable exhibition.

Reaching the stable where Thorpe was standing with Red Bannion, Duveen stared at them with his bloodshot eyes and then he said to Bannion, "Saddle my horse and be damned quick about it."

Bannion looked at him for a moment and then walked into the stable. Major Duveen stood there, his heavy legs spread, the jaw still thrust out, glaring at Thorpe. Then he said flatly, "Who killed my wife?"

Thorpe looked at him and then at Welch who was standing to one side.

"Reckon I found two of them," Thorpe said, "but there was a third one that got away."

Bennett Duveen said in a low voice, "Durango."

Thorpe's eyes flicked but he said nothing. Nate Welch said, "No use ridin' hell for leather, major. You still ain't sure Durango did it."

"He was out to get me," Duveen rasped, "one way or the other. I'm not waiting until he puts a bullet in my back."

Thorpe said to Horner, "Three of them took Mrs. Duveen from the stage. One of them peeled off."

Horner nodded. "We picked up his trail but lost it again when he turned back into the stage road a mile north of Benton."

Bannion came out with Duveen's big chestnut and the major hauled himself up into the saddle. As he did so Thorpe saw the gun stuck in his waistband. He rode away hard, heading toward Benton.

Red Bannion had come out and was looking at Nate Welch, waiting for Welch to give the order for them to ride after the major as had been the custom, but this time Welch said nothing. He stood there, his green eyes narrowed, his big chin thrust out, his spade-like hands on his hips, and his head cocked slightly to one side—as he watched Duveen ride off to his death.

Horner looked at Welch and then at Thorpe. Without a word the sheriff stepped into the saddle and rode off, going on after the major.

Bannion spat and said, "Reckon he ain't comin' back, is he, Nate?"

"How in hell would I know?" Welch snapped and he turned and walked back toward the ranch house.

Bannion said, "Reckon that's the way it is. Duveen pulls a gun on Durango an' he's dead, an' now Nate Welch don't give a damn. Maybe he figures with Mrs. Duveen dead, too, he walked into what's left?"

"Left of what?" Thorpe asked him.

Bannion shrugged. "Damned if I know," he said. "I just hear there was plenty a while back."

"Army payroll money," Thorpe said. "Is that what it was?"

Bannion looked at him. "Reckon I only hear things," he smiled, "an' I could hear wrong sometimes."

As Thorpe led the tired black gelding into the stable, Bannion said, "You lettin' Durango take him?"

Thorpe looked at the redhead for a moment and then he said flatly, "You figure he's supposed to be taken?"

"It ain't mine to say," Bannion grinned.

Thorpe pulled the saddle off the black and carried it over to a dapple gray in one of the stalls. He put the saddle on the gray and rode off, heading after Horner and Duveen.

There wasn't any doubt in his mind now that Major Duveen was going to die and there was nothing anybody could do about it if they wanted to, not Horner, not himself. He'd seen it in Duveen's eyes. The major was determined to die. He'd been through hell; his wife was dead, and he wanted no more of it, except perhaps to see Durango dead first. If he didn't die tonight he'd die tomorrow or the next day. Thorpe was confident that Major Bennett Duveen, with some sixteen dead men on his conscience, would not rest until he'd settled something in his mind.

Up ahead, as the light faded from the sky, Thorpe saw Horner riding with Duveen now, trying to remonstrate with him, but Duveen was riding on at a fast pace, apparently not even listening.

Thorpe made no effort to catch up with them. He'd had no sleep since the previous night and he was feeling it. He told himself that he was a damn fool for riding back to Benton. Duveen had been responsible for Tom Halloran's death and Duveen deserved to die. He could not bring himself to kill Duveen, though. The major was no gunman and now he was drunk and would remain drunk. It would be like killing a sheep.

It was nearly dark when they reached Benton and Duveen headed straight for the Alhambra, dismounting there. Horner dismounted, also, and seeing Thorpe come up now, he waited on the porch.

Duveen had gone inside, and as Thorpe came up on the porch he looked inside and saw the major up at the bar, still hatless, his wide face flushed and big shoulders set tight.

Horner said to Thorpe, "How the hell can a man carry that much liquor?"

"You can't stop it," Thorpe told him.

"Reckon I can stop three men from jumping one," Ben Horner observed, "an' that's what I figure on doin'."

"Durango in there?" Thorpe asked.

Horner shook his head. "The major might not find him until he's sobered up."

"Not in this world," Thorpe observed. "The major's aiming to die drunk and he'll do it."

As he spoke he saw three riders moving up the main street of Benton, riding at a leisurely pace, and he recognized the man in the middle as the tall, gaunt, long-jawed Durango, with the blue-veined hands and the cold blue eyes.

The three men headed in toward the tie rack in front of the Alhambra and dismounted. They tied the horses and came up onto the porch. Ben Horner said flatly, looking at the two men with Durango, "Reckon you boys can stay outside."

"What in hell for?" the short stubby man with the round face asked querulously.

"Just stay out," Horner told him.

Durango looked at Horner and then at Thorpe and then he stepped to the doors to look inside. The light from inside fell across his lean, angular face, the cruel hawk's nose, the narrow chin. Seeing Duveen at the bar, hatless, alone, with a bottle in front of him, a cold smile slid across the gunman's face.

The second man with him with the slanted oriental eyes said peevishly, "Ain't no lawman tellin' me when I can drink an' when I can't."

Horner said quietly, "I'm tellin' you, mister."

"I'm telling you, too," Thorpe added.

Durango said easily, "Stay put, Lafe." He looked at Thorpe steadily for one moment, and then as if satisfied, walked on past him into the saloon.

Thorpe looked in over the doors to make sure that Hallie was not there and then he waited. It reminded him of the time when as a boy they'd been preparing to slaughter a hog. He had the same feeling.

Durango moved between the tables leisurely, pulling up at an empty space a half-dozen feet from where Duveen was doing his drinking. There were two drinkers in between them, and, as Durango called for a bottle, one of the men moved away from the bar.

The second man remained a few minutes longer and then he, too, walked off. Durango turned to face Duveen, his left elbow resting on the wood, the big gun on his hip clear, that same cold smile on his face.

Duveen was lifting a shot glass to his mouth when he saw Durango in the bar mirror. There was no hesitation on the major's part whatever. Dropping the glass, he swung, his right hand moving toward the gun in his waistband. He had the gun out, the muzzle swinging up toward Durango when Durango's first bullet struck him in the chest.

Duveen's gun dropped in his hand and he took a step backward. The second slug caught him lower down. He still stood up, though, a rock of a man, staring at Durango, the hatred in his bloodshot eyes. Now he struggled to bring the gun up to shooting position, but his strength was gone.

The gun dropped from his hand, striking the brass foot rail with a ringing sound. Duveen then swung around, his back toward the bar, both elbows on the wood and slid down slowly to a sitting position, pain coming to his eyes. He sat back against the bar, closing his eyes like a child and he held both hands over his stomach. Thorpe saw the blood begin to trickle down between his fingers.

Sheriff Horner pushed in through the doors, moving through the stunned crowd which had started to seek cover. Two of the bartenders joined Horner as he crouched down beside Duveen.

As the two bartenders carried the major toward a back room, Ben Horner following, Durango walked toward the door, pushing out onto the porch where Thorpe was waiting.

Thorpe said to him, "That was an easy one."

"They're all easy," Durango said and he walked to his horse, the two men with him following.

Thorpe went into the Alhambra and back to the rear room where Duveen had been taken. He saw Hallie Grant coming down the stairs and when she saw him in the crowd an expression of relief swept over her face.

Thorpe nodded to her and went on into the back room. They'd placed the major on a cot and one of the bartenders was loosening his shirt, but looking at him Thorpe could see that it was only a matter of minutes before Duveen died. Already, the major's eyes had a strange, faraway look.

A man called into the room, "We're gettin' Doc Prescott."

Horner looked at Thorpe and shrugged, indicating that he, too, realized that it was hopeless. Duveen looked up at Horner for a moment in silence and then motioned for him to come closer. His voice was very weak and Thorpe, at the door, could not even hear what he was saying to the lawman, who now knelt down on one knee beside the cot.

It was several minutes before Doctor Prescott arrived with his bag, and Duveen still spoke with Horner as the physician opened his bag and took out his instruments.

The major died before the doctor could even examine him. His head fell back and his eyes opened all the way. Horner stood up, a strange expression on his face as he turned around.

As the sheriff walked toward the door he looked at Thorpe and said quietly, "Know what he said?"

Thorpe nodded and he saw Horner's eyebrows lift.

"Duveen was behind the raid on the paymaster's wagon up at Landers," Thorpe said. "He planned it and collected most of the money."

Horner nodded. "He cleared young Lieutenant Tom Halloran," he said. "There's been some talk in this part of the country that Halloran knew a lot more about the holdup than he should have known."

"I know," Thorpe said. "Tom Halloran was my brother."

Again, Ben Horner stared at him. "That why you're here?" he asked.

Thorpe nodded. "What about the others? Who was in with him?"

"Welch," Horner stated. "Durango. That's why Durango's here. The haul was a lot bigger than he'd thought it was. There were others, smaller fry, and they were all paid off. I figure there were a lot of others in the band beginning to push Duveen. Farnham was in with the bunch and Duveen wanted him out of the territory."

Thorpe said softly, "Durango was one of them. You want Durango tonight?"

"I'll take him," Horner said.

Thorpe was shaking his head. "Tom Halloran was my brother," he stated. "Reckon that puts me in it, sheriff." He had another thought. "What about his wife?" he asked. "She know?"

Horner nodded. "Mrs. Duveen found out the past day or so. Maybe Duveen talked in his sleep; maybe she ran across something. There were bank books. Duveen was smart enough to keep most of the money in Chicago banks under an assumed name. All these hardcases who were pushing him didn't know that. Even Welch didn't know it. They figured he'd be afraid to try to bank that kind of cash without arousing suspicion, but he did it by depositing in several banks."

"When she found out she wanted to leave," Thorpe said. "Duveen tried to hold her. I think he really loved her in spite of all their troubles."

"When she was killed," Horner said, "he didn't want any more of it—not the money, not anything."

"Welch knew she was trying to run out," Thorpe told him. "He was watching the hotel. When she tried to get out of town he went after her with two dogs to whom he'd paid big money. He never told the major about it because he knew Duveen wouldn't go so far as to kill her. He had to have her killed to protect himself. If she'd started to talk he'd hang."

They went back into the bar room where Hallie was waiting.

"Is he dead?" Hallie asked quietly.

Thorpe nodded. "It was Durango," he said. "Duveen wanted to die. He came here for that reason." He looked at Horner, then, and he said, "The major admitted he'd raided the paymaster's wagon with a bunch of cut-throats dressed as Indians. Durango and Welch were part of the crew."

"I'll be going up to Fort Landers in a day or two," Horner said, "to straighten things out with them."

Hallie said to Thorpe, "And you're going after Durango and Welch?"

Thorpe looked at her. "They helped kill my brother," he said.

Hallie looked toward the door out of which they'd just come. "He's dead," she said. "You know that."

Thorpe smiled. "We know it," he admitted.

The doctor came out of the room to speak a word to Ben Horner, and while they were alone for a moment Hallie said to Thorpe, "Now you've settled it you'll ride on again."

Thorpe shook his head. “A man doesn’t have to go forever,” he said. “I’ll be back.”

“Come alive,” Hallie told him. “You’re no good to any woman dead.”

“I figure I’ll be alive,” Thorpe said and he touched her hand and went outside with Horner.

“Welch is out at D-Bar,” Thorpe said. “I figure Durango went out that way after shooting the major. He might want to have a look around.”

“He’s a damned fool if he figures the money is out there,” Horner said. “All of them were damned fools.”

When they were stepping into the saddles Horner said thoughtfully, “Will Duveen’s riders back up Welch?”

“No,” Thorpe told him. “They’ll let him handle this one alone when they know Duveen is dead.”

“That means Welch is dead, too,” Horner observed.

“Dead as hell,” Thorpe agreed. “He can’t stand up to Durango.”

Horner rubbed his jaw. “Who can?” he asked, the worry in his voice.

X

Thorpe and Ben Horner rode out of Benton heading toward D-Bar, but as they were passing the last dilapidated shack on the street a rifle cracked from the corner of the building. Thorpe had been reaching forward to adjust one of the reins and he felt the breath of the bullet across his shoulders.

Horner gasped as the slug struck him. The sheriff slumped forward in the saddle, and then slid to the ground.

Pulling the Colt gun from the holster, Thorpe fired one shot toward the building and then slipped to the ground, keeping the gray horse in between himself and the bushwhacker.

He could hear a man running down the alley but he couldn't see him. With Horner on the ground he was unable to take up the pursuit immediately.

Ben Horner lay on his side as Thorpe ran up to him. One leg was moving back and forth and he was muttering something under his breath.

"See him?" the sheriff gasped.

"He's gone," Thorpe said. "You hit bad, sheriff?"

"In the side," Ben Horner told him. "It ain't killin' me."

There were people coming up the street now,

and Thorpe said to one of them, as he straightened up, "Get Doc Prescott."

Thorpe then started running down the walk toward the center of town. The ambusher had undoubtedly run down behind the row of buildings along the street, which meant that eventually he would be slipping out into the street.

Thorpe ran at top speed past astonished townspeople. He realized that there was only a small possibility he would see a man coming out of an alley or side street, and be able to identify him as the one who'd fired on them from the shack.

Still running, he went past the Alhambra Saloon. Just beyond was the alley in which the attempted killer of Major Duveen had crouched that first night Thorpe had been in town.

As Thorpe raced toward the alley now, Nate Welch suddenly stepped out into the patch of light from the law office. Seeing Thorpe driving straight toward him, Welch suddenly stopped and stared.

He had a gun on his hip, but he made no attempt to draw it as he whirled and dashed back into the alley. Thorpe took after him, knowing beyond any doubt now that Welch had been the man who'd fired that rifle shot. It had been written across his face in haggard lines.

Even as Thorpe raced into the alley, though, he was wondering why? Why had Nate Welch fired at him from ambush? He was positive that shot had been directed at him and not at Ben Horner.

When Welch reached the far end of the alley he paused and his gun winked again in the darkness. Hugging the wall, Thorpe sent one bullet back at him, but could not tell whether his lead had gone home or not.

He kept running forward and when he reached the end of the alley he could hear Welch running hard across the vacant lots behind the buildings. He caught a glimpse of the D-Bar ramrod tearing through a patch of light about thirty yards away.

Now Welch turned and fired again to keep him at a distance. When Thorpe returned the fire Welch let out a yell. Then he darted off again, weaving this time and dragging his right leg.

There was a pile of debris just beyond a low fence, and Welch scrambled over the fence and dropped down behind the mound. Knowing that he was going to open fire, Thorpe leaped into the rear doorway of a house just as a bullet from Welch's gun smashed into the door frame.

Gun in hand, Thorpe dropped to his knees and fired twice around the entrance way. He pulled back as Welch returned the fire.

At the other end of the building in which he was now concealed, Thorpe could hear a woman crying in alarm. A baby had been awakened by the shooting and it, too, was wailing in fright.

Nate Welch lay still behind the hummock and

Thorpe realized that he was more dangerous now, wounded, than he'd been before. Moving farther back into the house Thorpe located a door off the darkened corridor into which he'd come.

He turned the door knob and entered the room, which was dark and smelling of leather. The room apparently was a leather store room for the saddlemaker's shop up front.

Pushing in between the piles of leather, Thorpe stepped to a window which looked out on the rear yard, a window which gave him a much better angle on Nate Welch behind the pile of debris.

He stepped up to the dusty window carefully and looked out through the glass. He could see the hummock not more than ten yards away, and in the dim light he could even see a portion of Welch's body sprawled behind it, gun drawn, waiting for Thorpe to reveal himself in the doorway.

For several long moments Thorpe stood at the window, looking out, and then very deliberately he raised the barrel of the gun and poked out the glass in one of the panes.

As the window pane shattered, Nate Welch jerked his body around and fired twice, the lead smashing through the unbroken panes of glass, inches away from where Thorpe stood.

Thorpe fired through the broken pane. He sent one shot and Welch's body seemed to jump as the bullet took him. Welch came up on his knees and then incredulously started to crawl away on hands and knees like a dog. He moved quite quickly at first, but before he'd gone more than a dozen feet he collapsed and lay still.

Moving out into the yard, the gun in his hand, Thorpe walked toward him slowly. When he saw Welch's gun laying on the ground behind the hummock, the starlight glinting on the metal, he holstered his own gun.

Nate Welch wasn't quite dead. When Thorpe rolled him over, the D-Bar ramrod was mumbling something under his breath. Kneeling down, Thorpe said quietly, "A damn fool business, Nate, throwing lead at me from an alley."

"Had to," Welch panted. "You're another Halloran, Lieutenant's brother. Ain't you?"

"Who told you?" Thorpe asked.

"Man in town recognized you as Thorpe Halloran," Welch muttered. "I'd seen your brother an' I put the pieces together. You came down here to learn something an' you learned too damned much."

"That shot was meant for me, not for Horner," Thorpe said quietly.

"For you," Welch mumbled. "Now Duveen's gone an' I'm gone an' only Durango is left, an' all that damned money back at the ranch. I know it's under the floor. He keeps it under the floor. All that damn money!"

There was envy and greed and regret in his voice as he died.

Thorpe stood up, looking down at him. Welch had died trying to get possession of a great deal of money which Major Duveen had placed in Chicago banks. It was something Welch hadn't known and Durango didn't know. Durango now was out at D-Bar to search for the money, ready to kill again for something he would never have.

Back on the main street Thorpe found two men carrying Horner into his office nearby. Doc Prescott, a harried little man, bustled in to extract the bullet which had gone in under Horner's ribs.

Horner looked up at Thorpe, the pain in his eyes, and he said, "Welch is dead?"

Thorpe nodded.

"Saves us the trouble of hanging him," Horner muttered, his eyes closed. "What about Durango?"

"I'll see him," Thorpe said.

"Three of them," Horner told him, his eyes still closed.

"I know," Thorpe nodded. He was thinking that all three probably had been in that raid on the paymaster's wagon.

"Careful," Horner said. "You'd be smart to wait."

"Waiting's over," Thorpe told him, and he went out into the street.

He was in no condition to go after anyone else tonight, though. His body was lax and his brain was dull. He needed sleep before he went up against men like Durango and his two riders. He'd been in the saddle the entire night chasing Lauren Duveen's killers far to the north, and he hadn't slept since the night before. He had to sleep now.

Hallie was standing out in front of the Alhambra when he came up and he stopped in front of her.

"Who was it?" she asked.

"Welch," he told her. "He'd figured out who I was and he knew I'd be coming after him."

"And that leaves only Durango," she said, "and Horner can't help you."

"Horner can't help anyone for a while," Thorpe agreed.

"You're not going out tonight?"

Thorpe shook his head. "Figured I'd stay at the hotel and sleep some."

"I'll fix you a supper first," Hallie said. "Come inside." Wearily, Thorpe went into the Alhambra with her and upstairs to her apartment. He lay on a couch in the living room while she busied herself in the tiny kitchen at the rear. He was asleep when she finally called him, but he was hungry. He sat in the kitchen with Hallie watching him across the table, and he consumed the steaks and fried potatoes she'd made for him.

"You've always gone it alone," she said. "Why? Now you have friends out at D-Bar. They'll help you."

"Durango is my job," Thorpe said. "Reckon that's why I came up here."

"Three against one," Hallie reminded him, "and I don't want to see you dead."

"I don't aim to be dead," Thorpe smiled at her.

When he'd finished eating he got up and he said, "I'll be at the hotel."

She looked at him, standing across from him as he stood by the table, and then she came into his arms.

"You're a fool," she said softly, "but I want you to stay alive—for me."

He kissed her gently and then he stepped around her to the door. "I'll be back," he told her and he went out.

At the hotel he took a room on the second floor, locked the door, kicked off his boots, and was asleep almost as soon as his head touched the pillow.

When he awoke the sun was streaming into the room. He washed and shaved, and when he went downstairs to have his breakfast in the hotel dining room, he found Baines and Bannion sitting in the lobby waiting for him.

Thorpe looked at them suspiciously. "Who sent for you?" he asked.

Bannion shrugged. "Grant woman said you was here," he grinned. "Figured we'd stop in."

"She sent for you?" Thorpe asked him.

Bannion looked at Baines. "Said you was

here," he repeated, "an' that you figured on goin' after Durango. We're here, too."

"My fight," Thorpe told him. "You don't work for D-Bar any more. Duveen is dead."

"An' Welch we hear, too," Leo Baines said. "Durango come out to D-Bar last night an' turned the damn place upside down. Lookin' for greenbacks, I'd say."

"He didn't find anything," Thorpe told him. "The money is in Chicago."

Baines shook his head. "All the damn fools," he said. "They should o' figured Duveen wouldn't be that dumb to keep it in sight."

"Where's Durango now?" Thorpe wanted to know.

Baines shrugged. "Three of 'em rode off, but I'm figurin' they're stayin' around awhile. Durango's got it in his head that the money's here somewhere. He ain't ridin' away from it."

"We ain't ridin' away, either," Red Bannion said, looking at Thorpe thoughtfully.

"All you might get from this job is a bullet through the head," Thorpe told him. "You're a damned fool, Red."

"We'll stick around," Bannion smiled. "Go eat your breakfast now. Any time Durango turns up you'll know about it."

Thorpe went into the dining room and he was eating when a boy brought the word that Sheriff Horner wanted to see him. Baines and Bannion were sprawled in chairs on the porch when he went outside. He walked up the street toward the sheriff's office.

Horner was sitting in bed, but his face was pale and drawn as Thorpe came into the room, indicating that he'd had a bad night.

"Still figure on goin' after Durango?" Horner asked him.

Thorpe nodded.

"Why not do it legal?" Horner said. "I could swear you in."

"You want me to bring him back?" Thorpe smiled.

Horner looked at him. "That's the law," he said.

"You know damn well Durango will never come," Thorpe told him, "Not alive."

"It still should be done legal," Horner said stubbornly. "I want to swear you in."

Thorpe nodded. "You're the law in this town," he said.

When he left the office ten minutes later he had a five-pointed star pinned to his shirt. He came back to the hotel porch where Bannion and Baines were sitting, and Bannion said, "So Horner wants it cut an' dried, an' everything wrapped up nice."

"That's the way it is," Thorpe told him.

"You're not wrappin' anything up with Durango," Leo Baines smiled. "His kind wasn't born to hang. When he goes out he aims to take somebody with him for company."

"We'll see," Thorpe said. "I'm riding out now."

Both Bannion and Baines stood up. "We might mosey along," Bannion said, "just to keep you company."

"Durango could be holed up down in Avalon," Baines said, "only you couldn't be sure about it. There's no tellin' where the hell he might be. He could have skipped out, too."

Thorpe was quite sure Durango hadn't skipped. Durango didn't know about the money, and he wouldn't ride off until he'd satisfied his curiosity about something else. Durango had to see how fast Thorpe Halloran's gun was, and he wouldn't be leaving until he knew about that. He was that breed of man.

XI

The three of them rode out of Benton at high noon, heading south, with Thorpe intending to stop at D-Bar first to see if Durango had returned before going on to the ghost town of Avalon.

"What in hell will happen to the ranch?" Bannion asked as they moved down the stage road.

"Bought with government money," Thorpe said. "Reckon the government will take it once Horner tells the army men up at Landers what happened to their payroll."

"Duveen winds up with a hole in the ground," Baines murmured, "an' not a damn thing more, after all his troubles."

"We're all windin' up there sooner or later," Bannion said.

When they reached D-Bar they found the hardcases preparing to pull out. Jug Hansen had his horse saddled and was ready to ride. Dave Shaw was going with him and they were pushing farther west into the mining country.

Thorpe said, "Durango been back, Jug?"

"Ain't seen him," Hansen said, and then he stared at the star on Thorpe's vest. "Reckon you're gettin' up in the world, mister," he grinned. "That's for Durango?"

“We’re picking him up,” Thorpe said, “one way or the other.”

“Luck,” Hansen nodded. “A man needs it sometimes.”

After they’d left, Thorpe rode on again with Bannion and Baines, moving south in the direction of Avalon. It was mid-afternoon when they came in sight of the town basking in the hot sunshine.

Nothing moved down in the street. There were no horses in sight at the racks, and no sounds whatever.

“Holin’ up somewhere else,” Bannion observed. “Reckon we kin ride in an’ have a look.”

They rode down into town carefully, guns drawn, but after looking into some of the alleys and empty stables Thorpe decided to give it up.

“Way I figure it,” Baines said, “Durango wants that money. He knows Duveen’s dead, but he don’t know about Welch, an’ he might be figurin’ Welch knows where it is. He’ll be lookin’ for Welch—at D-Bar or in Benton.”

“Makes sense,” Thorpe agreed.

“He’ll be keepin’ out o’ sight, too,” Baines went on, “because he won’t be wantin’ to scare Nate off.”

They left Avalon, riding north again, and it was dusk when they entered Benton, pulling up at the hotel where Thorpe now had his room. They watched for Durango’s horse at the tie rack, but did not spot the animal. Thorpe remembered that he'd been riding a claybank.

They had their supper at the hotel and then moved down toward the Alhambra Saloon, finding it nearly empty at this early hour. Hallie said to Thorpe when he came in, "He hasn't been in town today. I've had people watching for him."

"He'll turn up," Thorpe said.

He played cards with Bannion and Baines till nearly eleven o'clock. Then Bannion got up and made a round of the saloons in town, coming back with word that Durango and his crew had not ridden in.

"Reckon we could be guessin' wrong," Baines said. "Maybe he did figure the money was gone an' he pulled out."

"You goin' after him, then?" Bannion asked, looking at Thorpe.

Thorpe nodded. He was getting restless now, positive that Durango was still in the vicinity but holed up, just biding his time. He'd never known a gun fighter of the caliber of Durango to run out on a fight, and Durango knew that a fight was due between them.

Sitting at the card table the thought was running through Thorpe's mind that Durango was waiting somewhere. Durango knew about Welch; Durango knew that he, Thorpe Halloran, was wearing a star and looking for a showdown with him; and now Durango was deliberately staying out of sight waiting until he could catch him alone.

The more Thorpe considered this matter the more feasible it became. Durango was no man's fool, and he'd met up with Bannion and Baines before. He wanted a little edge and he wouldn't have any kind of edge with the two D-Bar hard-cases in the fight. As a matter of fact it could be the other way around.

At midnight, Thorpe pushed the cards away. He said, "They could be riding in this minute and we'd never know it."

"Reckon we'd hear about it soon enough," Baines told him.

Thorpe shook his head. "Rather have you two boys posted at each end of town to spot them when they come. That way there's no mis-takes."

Red Bannion looked at Leo Baines, and then he shrugged. "That the way you want it," Bannion told him, "it's all right with me."

Baines pushed his hat back on his head. "Gittin' edgy?" he asked.

"That could be," Thorpe nodded. "I'll be out in front. When you spot them head back here quick."

When the two gunhands had gone out he had a drink at the bar and chatted with Hallie for a few moments before going outside.

"If they've cleared out of the country," Hallie

said, “it’s all the better. Somebody will catch up with him sooner or later.”

“I’ll catch up with him,” Thorpe said and he downed his drink, touching her hand lightly before walking out onto the porch.

Out at D-Bar earlier in the day, Thorpe had shifted his saddle to the black gelding in the stable, and the black was now tied at the rack between two other horses.

Untying the animal, he walked down the side street adjacent to the Alhambra, making no attempt to conceal himself. If Durango were watching from a building in town he could easily see his man pulling out.

At the other end of the street Thorpe stepped into the saddle and rode off, making a wide sweep of the town and heading south. He listened carefully as he rode along but could hear nothing.

A mile beyond Benton he turned back into the stage road and headed south which would take him in the general direction of D-Bar and Avalon. He had the feeling as he rode that he was getting near the end of the trail—a trail which had started almost a year ago when he’d heard of Tom’s death and the rumors had begun to seep across the border.

He rode on into the night with the stars shining down on him, and the knowledge that tonight he had a woman waiting for him back in Benton. It had never been this way before and he wondered how it would affect him when the lead began to fly. A man could be too careful, too anxious to live, and that kind of man usually died.

Two miles out of Benton he heard the horses coming up behind him, and when he turned and looked back he saw three riders just coming up over a rise in the road. The ruse had worked. Durango *had* been watching somewhere in town.

Touching his spurs to the black, Thorpe pushed ahead faster, but the three men behind him picked up speed, also. The odds were now three to one and Durango liked this a lot better. He would stay with this situation all night now until it was over.

Thorpe rode due south, knowing where he was going. Ahead of him lay Avalon, the ghost town where George Varney had sought refuge and where he had died. Who would die tonight?

The black was running smoothly and strongly, keeping well ahead of the three riders behind. There were no shots fired as the distance was still too great for accurate shooting. He noticed as he glanced back that they'd spread out somewhat, in case he did open up with his pistol.

It was another hour's ride out to Avalon and Thorpe let the black horse run. Durango and his riders were making no attempt to catch up with him, and he wondered if they knew where he was going.

The black kept up the pace mile after mile, still running strongly. He had about a seventy-five-yard lead on the three riders behind him, and the black maintained it as the animal pounded into the main street of Avalon past the abandoned railroad station.

Slipping off the gelding's back, Thorpe darted into an alley adjacent to the hotel, the largest building in town, a two-story structure with a balcony surrounding the entire second floor.

As he stepped in through the side entrance to the hotel, he could hear Durango and his two riders coming into the main street.

Durango was calling sharply, "Pick him up! Pick him up!"

It was going to be a game now, a deadly game of hide-and-seek—and if he made one mistake he would be dead.

It was dark inside the hotel as Thorpe moved through what might have been the bar and then into the hotel lobby. Through a dusty window which looked out on the main street, he saw Durango and the two men down near the railroad station. They crossed the road and he lost sight of him. They'd seen him go into the alley next to the hotel and they were coming to ferret him out.

Moving across the lobby, Thorpe located the stairway and went up the stairs rapidly. Stepping into one of the rooms he moved over to a door which opened onto the balcony overlooking the main street.

The door was slightly ajar and he slipped outside, crouching down out of sight. There were no sounds in the town and nothing moved.

Below him now he heard a board give as a man put his weight on it. Listening carefully, he heard a rusted door hinge squeak. They were coming into the hotel.

On hands and knees behind the balcony railing, Thorpe crawled to the corner of the balcony and sat down in such a position that he could face both the front of the building and the one side. He sat there with the Colt gun in his lap.

Below him he could hear slight sounds inside the building as Durango and his men made a careful search. Through a broken window nearby he heard a man say in a low voice, "Reckon he ain't in this one. Must o' gone down the street a ways."

A few moments later the door through which Thorpe had come out onto the balcony was pushed open cautiously, and then a man came out. It was the short fellow with the round face and the flattened nose.

He didn't see Thorpe in the shadows at the other end of the balcony as Thorpe sat very still on the floor. With the gun braced on his knee Thorpe said easily, "This way, friend."

The short man was carrying his gun in his hand. He whirled, and the roar of his gun blended with Thorpe's as they both fired together. Very neatly, Thorpe's hat was lifted from his head by the bullet. His own slug caught the short fellow in the chest, bouncing him back against the door frame. He caught onto the door as he started to go down, held on to it tight, and pulled it from the hinges with a crash. He lay there with the door on top of him, one arm hanging out between the balcony supports.

Picking up his hat, Thorpe stepped out over the balcony rail and lowered himself rapidly to the ground on one of the balcony pillars. Running fast, he crossed the road and darted into the open doorway of a store. The windows of the store had been boarded up over the broken glass.

Even as he leaped in through the doorway, a gun banged from one of the hotel windows and the bullet struck the door frame. Stepping toward the window he looked out between the boards, watching the hotel front across the way. Up on the balcony he saw the arm of the stubby man.

He stood there watching the hotel. There were only two of them left, but he knew Durango was not giving it up. They knew where he'd gone now, but they were not positive that he was still in the same building. For this reason the advantage lay with him. He could move from house to house, from alley to alley, and it was their job to locate him if they wanted him dead.

The signboard was squeaking again up the street. Off in the hills he could hear a coyote barking. Suddenly a gun opened up from the lobby of the hotel and bullets began to rip through the window boards.

Thorpe threw himself to the floor, flattening his body out on the wood. He lay there after the barrage had stopped and he knew that if he'd remained on his feet one of those bullets would have gone through his body.

He stood up now and looked through the crack again, knowing that there was only a small possibility that they would again fire at random at the window. He saw the tall fellow with the oriental eyes, whom Durango had addressed as Lafe, dart out of the alley a short distance up the street and cross over.

Lafe was planning on coming up on him from the rear while Durango kept him occupied at the front of the house. Hurriedly, Thorpe moved to the rear of the building, and went out through the rear door.

Lafe was now on his side of the street, either coming down an alley or slipping through the buildings. Gun in hand, Thorpe moved down along the rear of the houses in the direction from which he expected Lafe to come.

He flattened himself against the wall as he approached an alley, hearing Lafe running up the other end. He waited now in the shadows against the wall as Lafe swung around the corner of the building, his body brushing against Thorpe's as he ran.

Immediately realizing that he'd come upon his man, Lafe yelled out loud as he jerked his body around, trying to bring his gun up for a shot. Thorpe slashed hard with the barrel of his gun at Lafe's head, but the blow was a slanting one, catching him on the side of the ear and the shoulder.

Lafe went down partially stunned, but even as he fell he was opening up with his gun, shooting wildly. One bullet clipped Thorpe's left boot. Lafe rolled, trying to get off another hurried shot, but Thorpe's bullet took him through the forehead, and he fell back with a sudden soft cry.

Thorpe looked around for one moment and then crossed the yard, stepped over a broken-down fence. He slid down a small embankment to the abandoned railroad switching yard and headed back along rusted tracks toward the railroad station, shoving cartridges into the empty chambers of the gun as he walked.

Durango had heard the shots and he heard the shout, and when Lafe did not appear he would know it was now a case of one against one.

Stepping across the tracks Thorpe went up on the loading platform at the rear of the station and then moved cautiously toward the street. Keeping back in the shadows, he looked up toward the hotel but saw nothing moving.

For a while he sat down on a bench in the

shadows, the gun across his lap, waiting, out of sight of the hotel. He calmly rolled a cigarette and lit, smoking it through before moving up to the street again to look out.

Twenty minutes had passed since he'd had it out with Lafe, but still Durango hadn't come out into the open. The three horses the men had ridden into town were still tied up out in front of the station, and if Durango intended to leave Avalon he'd have to come this way to get his horse. In another hour the light would be coming into the sky, and Thorpe was positive Durango would make his play before that happened.

Pulling back again, he stepped inside the railroad station with its dust-covered benches and rusted pot-bellied stove. There was a caged window on one side where the ticket seller had sold tickets.

The door leading into the office was open and Thorpe now walked toward it, looking inside. Chairs and desks lay tumbled on the floor together with papers scattered around them.

Picking up a three-legged stool, he placed it in front of the grated window. Taking out the Colt gun he lay it on the counter in front of him and then he sat down on the stool facing the door through which Durango would come if he entered this building. He imagined that Durango was moving through town, working his way through one building after the other. It would only be a matter of time before he came to the railroad station.

Thorpe sat on the stool, his arms resting on the wood. Another fifteen minutes passed and the first light was coming into the sky, creeping in through the dusty window, when he heard the light step on the boards outside.

He could hear Durango moving around the far side of the building, and he sat very still, the gun in his hand. Again he heard the steps. He saw Durango's shadow at the window, but he knew that the gunman could not see him sitting in the deep shadows near the window.

The door knob turned very gently, the hinges squeaking, as Durango came in, a gun in his hand. Durango looked around the room cautiously and then stepped inside, leaving the door ajar.

Outside, Thorpe could hear the three horses stamping restlessly. Durango now saw the second door leading into the office, and he walked across the floor passing within eight feet of the grilled window where Thorpe was waiting.

Gently, Thorpe called to him, "Here's your ticket, Durango, to hell."

Durango's gun hand moved like the head of a snake. His gun roared but Thorpe had moved his body away from the window as he spoke and the slug grazed one of the metal bars of the grate, making it ring hollowly.

Thorpe's bullet struck Durango above the belt

buckle, staggering him. As he fell he fired again, wildly now, his bullet smashing into the wall above the grate.

Thorpe's gun spoke a second time, the bullet taking Durango in the chest as he was trying to straighten up. It knocked him six feet back against the far wall. His body struck the wall and he slid down to a sitting position, the big Navy Colt sliding from his hand, his head falling down on his chest.

Before he died he managed to lift his head toward the grilled window, and he said in a low, sick voice, "Damn you, mister."

Then he fell over on his side and lay still.

Thorpe came out from the office to have a look. There were streaks of red and gold in the sky to the east, and the thin light was filtering through the windows as he looked down at the man.

He stepped outside now and sat down on the bench, watching the sun come up, and it was good to see it. He expected to see many more.

It was mid-morning when he rode into Benton, seeing the disappointed Red Bannion and Baines waiting for him on the hotel porch.

Baines said, "Had to handle it yourself."

Thorpe nodded. "All over," he said. "I'm obliged."

"For nothing," Bannion told him. "Man like you don't need nobody."

Thorpe didn't know that. He moved on to the

Alhambra where he found Hallie Grant having a cup of coffee at one of the tables. A bartender worked around the bar behind her.

When Thorpe came in he saw the light come into her eyes.

"You're back," she said, as he dropped wearily into the chair across from her.

"I'm back," Thorpe said.

"For good?" she wanted to know.

"For good." He smiled.

Hallie turned and said to the bartender, "Dan, can you bring another cup of coffee."

Thorpe sat there just looking across at her.

"And your business is finished," Hallie said.

Thorpe nodded. He picked up the coffee cup when the bartender brought it to him.

"This is a nice town to stay in," Hallie said, smiling.

Thorpe smiled back at her over the rim of the cup. "Reckon it is," he said. He meant it.

Center Point Large Print
600 Brooks Road / PO Box 1
Thorndike, ME 04986-0001 USA

(207) 568-3717

US & Canada:
1 800 929-9108
www.centerpointlargeprint.com